WELCOME TO RED CEDAR

"Your dad's the draft-dodger, right?"

"You got a name?" said Border.

"My name, you stinking son of a worthless traitor, is Bryan. My uncle used to be in school with your dad, and he says your dad fried his brains with drugs. He says your dad oughta be forgiven for running from the draft cuz he was so drug-soaked he didn't know what he was doing."

"He knew."

"That's what I think. I also think that when we start dropping bombs on Saddam, we oughta send his brainless, gutless body along."

"You want to talk brains, Bryan?" Border said cheerfully. "Well, I bet yours wouldn't fill a nut cup."

Border moved first, so Bryan's fist and knee collided with the locker.

HOMETOWN

Marsha Qualey

AN AVON FLARE BOOK

AVON BOOKS
A division of
The Hearst Corporation
1350 Avenue of the Americas
New York, New York 10019

Copyright © 1995 by Marsha Qualey
Published by arrangement with Houghton Mifflin Company
Visit our website at http://AvonBooks.com
Library of Congress Catalog Card Number: 94-49321
ISBN: 0-380-72921-0
RL: 6.7

First Avon Flare Printing: April 1997

AVON FLARE TRADEMARK REG. U.S. PAT. OFF. AND IN OTHER COUNTRIES, MARCA
REGISTRADA, HECHO EN U.S.A.

Printed in the U.S.A.

RA 10 9 8 7 6 5 4 3 2

HOMETOWN

I

Departure

Pyroball —

They never should have let the kid play. He was too little and new. He hadn't been hanging around long enough to get the feel of the game, to understand the timing and learn the moves.

The kid held the tennis ball too long. Worse, he gave it a squeeze, and a trickle of alcohol slid down his wrist. The flame followed, igniting the sleeve of his raggedy shirt.

He dropped the ball and howled. A girl screamed.

A bigger flame now. The kid shrieked.

Border Baker slipped out of his leather jacket and ran to the burning boy. "Sit down," he barked. The kid dropped to his knees, and Border covered the arm with the jacket, wrapped it tight until the flame was smothered.

The air stank.

Others crowded around them. The kid fell over and Border held him. "Kid, do you live with your folks?" The boy nodded. "Someone call them. Who knows his folks?"

No one did.

He looked at the boy and said, "Passed out." He rocked the boy. "You'll be okay, kid. It'll be okay."

They carried him to the emergency room at Presbyterian.

3

Ten blocks with dead weight. The boy groaned, but didn't come around. Border had an arm under the kid's back and a hold of his good hand. The burned one flopped loose. No one would touch it.

Sunday morning, 2 A.M., and it was slow in the E.R. The Saturday night drunks and brawlers had been sent home. Two women with babies, a man with an ice pack on his face, no other emergencies. The admission clerk rolled her head away from the TV and said, "Yeah, kids?"

"He's been burned," said Border. The clerk saw the hand and shouted. Suddenly the room was filled with adults doing their jobs.

Riley handed Border the leather jacket, murmured something, and all the kids fled. Border shrugged and found a chair. He was tired and he didn't mind answering questions. Hospitals, there were always questions. He'd even talk to the cops, if they came. It wasn't *his* tennis ball, *his* alcohol, *his* game, he could say. Yes, Officer, he knew they shouldn't play in the arroyos. Please, Officer, he'd only been there to find Riley, who owed him ten bucks.

"Riley, hey!" Border called, remembering. He twisted around. No kids anywhere. Ten-dollar loan to Riley. Dumb. Dumb as playing pyroball.

The clerk came with the questions. Border told what he knew, which was next to nothing.

"His parents? His address?"

Border shrugged.

"Then we'll just wait until he's awake," said the clerk. She went back to watching television, switching channels until she found news. A woman with incredible hair was interviewing generals in Saudi Arabia. The generals looked concerned. Manly. The reporter looked small. Border found a

4

Tootsie Roll in his jacket pocket, unwrapped it, and popped it into his mouth. He turned the leather jacket around in his hands, checking for damage. The silk lining was scorched, no worse.

Border zipped himself into the jacket, slunk down, and let the soft leather push up around his ears. He was in no hurry to leave. Anyway, where would he go? His dad might not even be at the apartment. "Let's leave at noon," the old man had said. "Please," Border had replied. "You're dragging me off to live in a strange place. Just let me have a couple more days with my friends." His father had been firm. "It's a long drive to Minnesota, and I want to have time to settle in before I start the new job." Border had walked out then, claiming he had to find Riley and the ten dollars.

Maybe he *had* left at noon, almost two days ago. Maybe this time he had shrugged off his son's disappearance into the streets of Albuquerque and left at noon. But he'd have had to make a phone call first. A call to Border's mother in Santa Fe.

"It's your problem this time. I give up. He's sixteen and doesn't think he needs a father. Fine. When you find him, you keep him." Maybe he had said that this time.

The calm and warmth of the hospital felt good. Border had spent Friday night at Dayton's apartment, a place where kids could always crash. But it had snowed — the first really cold night of the winter — so there were a lot of people at Dayton's. The music never stopped. Celeste was there with her baby. It cried, and she wanted to talk, anyone would do. With all that going on Border hadn't slept. Tonight he hadn't gone back, just sat in a diner with coffee and toast, asking for Riley anytime he saw someone he knew.

Someone did come in who knew about Riley. Said there

5

was a pyroball game going on up in Lobos Arroyo. Border bought the guy coffee and left, walked a mile in the cold. Ten dollars, after all.

Border tapped his fingers along his thighs. Wished he had his recorder. Stupid, he'd left without it. Left it on top of his duffle bag. He knew then his fate was sealed. He'd have to find his father. Without the instrument, he had no way to earn a living. "You win, Dad," he murmured. "I lose."

Defeated. Resigned. Tired.

He slept for hours in the waiting room chair and woke to find his father sitting next to him.

No smile? "Hey, Dad. Are we still leaving at noon?"

"If you're going to run and hide, you need to be smarter about it than to land in a hospital."

True enough. The old man was a nurse, an anesthetist, with lots of medical friends.

"Did someone around here call you?"

"I called. My kid disappears for two days, I check the hospitals. They told me you brought in a burned boy. One of your friends? Someone I know?"

"Just a kid."

His father tugged on Border's arm and they both rose. "I don't know why you all play that game," he said. "I don't know why the cops haven't stopped it, why they let it go on."

Border looked at the TV screen. Fighter jets were lined up on a Saudi Arabian tarmac. Lots of stuff was going on. Who knew why?

—◆—

Stalling tactic. "Maybe I should call Mom and say good-bye."

"You've said good-bye. And I doubt if you could reach her. When I was trying to find you, I called her. She said that the protest had been pushed up to this morning. She was scheduled to be in the first wave. It's almost sunrise. She's probably been arrested by now."

"Does she have bail money? She might need bail money, Dad."

"Not from me. Not this time."

Son and father walked to their car. Border wanted to ask his father to drive to Santa Fe, just an hour north, hardly out of the way. He wanted to drive by the capitol and see the protesters chained to the benches, see the bodies laid across the street. See his mother, if she hadn't already been hauled to jail.

He'd been at her apartment the night final protest plans had been voted upon. It had been packed, twenty adults screaming at each other because they were mad at the government. No guns for oil! We must be heard! Border had served tea and cookies, then, when business was done, agreed to play recorder for the remaining people. Seven minutes of Mozart. The protesters were old friends, sort of; his family had only lived in New Mexico three years. But they were like the friends they'd had everywhere. Fort Collins, Missoula, Detroit, Winnipeg, Toronto, though that was so long ago he couldn't remember.

Always friends in the apartment, on the phone, on the sofa.

When his mother and older half sister had moved to Santa Fe, he realized that most of the friends must have been theirs because the apartment became so quiet and empty.

He liked the quiet. He practiced more often, tackled Brahms. They bought a television.

Maybe she'd be on the news. "Dad, let's stay one more night."

"Where? I've turned in the apartment keys."

Border grinned. "Are we homeless?"

"No," his father responded sternly. "We have a home waiting in Minnesota."

The old man was willing to stay longer, just for breakfast. They both ordered big and ate it all. Border got seconds and coffee to go. Slipping on ice, he spilled half the cup before they were back in the car, then sloshed some on his pants as he set the cup on the dash. An ominous start, he said to his dad, who said nothing at all.

They reached the ramp onto the highway. Just before his father accelerated, Border looked back for a last glimpse of Albuquerque, his city. Out of the corner of his eye he glimpsed green hair come out of an apartment building.

A shout lodged in his throat: Dana! But no, of course not. His sister hadn't been in town for weeks and anyway, she was in South Carolina, visiting her father's family.

The city was slipping away. Beyond the highway, a child playing alone in the early morning hurled wet sand across a playground. Great brown gobs soared and fell, then hit the ground, scattering on impact.

—⚬—

For the first forty miles they listened to the radio, Border's father impatiently switching stations. War or football, that's all there was. Less than two weeks remained before the UN's ultimatum to Iraq expired. Three weeks until the Super Bowl. Announcers for either were deadly serious.

"Four teams prepare for today's battles; only two will survive."

"Tension is building among the troops waiting here at the Saudi border."

Border smiled. He liked hearing his name in the news. And for half a year he'd heard it plenty and seen it often in headlines.

Iraqi army crosses Kuwait's border.

Saddam's guns aimed at Saudi border.

Border towns wait in fear.

His favorite, though, was a headline his mother had clipped from the Santa Fe paper and sent without any added comment the day after hearing about a failed history test.

Latest poll: Border violation unacceptable.

Border drove through most of the night while his father slept. Progress was slow; the old car refused to go over sixty. They switched drivers somewhere in Oklahoma, and he slept for an hour before waking up to daylight and the flattest country he'd ever seen, flatter even than Manitoba.

They cleaned up at a rest stop. Border debated changing shirts, sniffed himself, decided it wouldn't be worth it.

South of Kansas City, snow started falling. Random flakes at first, then steadier and heavier. The sky behind them was a dark wall of clouds. Wind butted their car insistently.

North of Kansas City, the highway became snow-covered except for two dark tracks in the right lane.

They hadn't said much at all the entire trip and now they spoke less. A grunt from the father, soft music from the son as he hummed and tapped his fingers along his thighs in a deliberate pattern, recorder notes, a Telemann minuet.

They exited somewhere in Missouri, nearly skidding off the ramp. Three cars had gone off. Border looked for stranded travelers, but saw only empty vehicles and snow.

"Maybe the war began, they dropped the bombs, and we're the last ones left on earth," he joked. His father didn't smile. "Maybe the radiation is seeping down with the snow and destroying all life."

"Why are *we* alive?" his father grumbled.

"We're in a Volvo."

They found a town with a motel. "Free breakfast," Border read on the motel sign. He hoped for donuts.

They were given the last room. Could they share a bed? the clerk asked. Border grinned, his father nodded, the clerk took the credit card.

Border returned to the car to get their bags. He couldn't even see across the parking lot, and snow blanketed the car hood. He wrote a message with his finger.

Storm lashes Border.

Snowbound with Snowbirds —

They had a vending machine supper and then went to bed. His father slept while Border flipped channels. After midnight some of the movies got raunchy and Border watched, wondering. His father woke up briefly and looked at the screen.

10

"Turn it off," he commanded before falling back asleep.

Border obeyed; he'd seen enough.

When he woke, he dressed with stealth and went to find the free breakfast. The lobby was crowded with old people.

One man waved an arm. "This way, son," he called. "The food is over here."

Trapped now. All eyes on him. Border fixed a smile on his face and wove through the crowd until he reached the small kitchen at the end of the lobby.

Donuts and bagels, juice and coffee. Border took some of everything and found a chair next to the gas fireplace. When he had a mouthful of bagel, his face was shadowed. He looked up and saw the friendly man who'd hailed him.

Border rose, balancing things, and offered the man his chair.

"Goodness no, son. I suppose this table can hold me. Sit back down and eat. John Farmer."

Border tongued some cream cheese from behind a molar and let it slide down his throat before speaking. "Border Baker."

"Great galumphing boy, aren't you?"

This, Border decided, was one of those inane adult comments that required no response. He looked at his sneakers, size thirteen. He sipped juice.

John Farmer tried again. "Some storm, hey?"

Border sipped coffee.

"What I most want to know, son, is about your barber. Did he die on the job, or what?"

John Farmer got whacked on the shoulders.

A petite woman, with gray hair neatly knotted on the top of her head, winked at Border. "That's what you do if he

11

gets out of line." She sat on the table next to Border's inquisitor. "I'm Lil Devereaux."

"Don't be fooled, we're married. Six weeks now. She just wouldn't change her name."

His mate stole his coffee cup. "And neither would you, Farmer." They bantered on, touching each other gently.

"She's an artist," John Farmer said proudly. "A printmaker."

"My mother's an artist," Border said.

"He speaks!" said John Farmer, earning another whack.

Lil leaned forward. "What does she work in?"

They waited while he sipped more juice. "Performance."

John emitted a gleeful noise. "Is she one of those women who goes naked on stage?"

Whack.

The husband turned to the wife. "If I kept doing that to you, there'd be cops and judges and restraining orders."

"Then behave, Farmer, and I'll stop it."

"Nudity isn't a big part of her work," said Border, "but she's done it."

"Have you seen her do it, your own mother?"

"Twice."

John Farmer frowned. "That can't be healthy."

Border brushed crumbs off his chest. "I'd be happy if you'd write her and tell her that, Mr. Farmer."

"Just John, please. No one's ever called me Mister. Colonel, maybe. U.S. Army, retired."

"Is she a solo artist?" Lil asked.

Border nodded.

"What's her name?"

"Diana Morrison. She toured with her last show. Maybe you've heard of her?"

Lil shook her head.

"During the day she's a chemist."

"Goodness," said John Farmer. "What an interesting combination. Is she here? Where is she? I'd like to meet her."

"No, she's . . ." Whoa. In jail. "She's in Santa Fe. My father and I are moving to Minnesota."

The background noise was silenced when the front door opened and cold air and snow rolled in. The snow settled, revealing a motel employee carrying boxes of donuts. Two bags of oranges swung from his wrists.

"All the highways are closed, but Hinkley's market was open and I cleaned it out!"

Cheers rose to such a level that Border doubted anyone could still be sleeping in the motel. He excused himself, rose, and filled his coffee cup, then circulated around the room offering refills. When he returned the empty pot to the warmer, he found John Farmer brewing more.

"See that man, the one with the thin mustache?"

"Yes, Colonel."

"Call me John, or I'll get my wife to wallop you. That man's a barber, Border. He could finish the job."

Border ran one hand along the shaved side of his head, while his other tucked shoulder length locks behind an ear.

"You're moving to a new place, son. Might not be wise to make yourself an easy target. You can grow it back any way you want, after they get to know you."

Border considered the wisdom of this while looking at the television. Most everyone was watching. Someone had found a remote and switched from Desert Shield news to Regis and Kathie Lee. Regis was terrorizing a guest chef. All the women giggled, and the men seemed to be drifting toward naps. Border felt John Farmer's eyes on him.

"Morning, Border." His father's voice.

Border turned around and nodded, then resumed staring at the TV.

"Well, I'll be whipped," John Farmer said. "This is your father, I'll bet." He looked back and forth between father and son, measured the silence, and chuckled. "Good enough. We've got a long, snowy day ahead. Soon I'll know the story."

The Story —

If I felt like it, Colonel John Farmer, I guess I could tell quite a tale.

Family stories go back too far to see, so I'd have to say ours began when he ran.

My father was only nineteen when he ran from the United States to Canada. It was 1970 and he had received his draft induction notice. Vietnam waited. But my dad looked into his soul, or into his gut, and decided he couldn't do it. He stole money from his parents, stole his mother's car, and left the country.

A draft dodger.

He made his way to Toronto where he found plenty of other dodgers and deserters.

Still want to smile at him? Clap your hand on his back?

He found my mother there, too. She's from the U.S., but she had drifted into Canada, following a guy she thought she loved.

They met at a party back in 1973. One night in an apartment where dodgers were welcome to crash, someone spun out on bad acid. The trip got violent. Tables turned and glasses broke. People screamed and fled. My mother was unable to get out of the low sofa where she was nursing her baby, my half sister, Dana. She looked up into the mad face of the deranged deserter. She looked up at a knife.

It was my father who talked him down. In smooth, low tones, he brought the drug-bombed brain back to earth. He took the knife, handed it over to be put away, then took the man outside for a long walk and talk.

My mother remembered. And a month later when my father came looking for work at the bookstore she managed, she hired him, certain that he was a useful, reliable man.

They married twelve months later, after I was born.

Then, a succession of shared apartments with other dodgers and their women and kids. Jobs that never paid much. Toronto, my parents decided, was getting too hard on Americans. Too mean. They moved to Winnipeg and breathed easier on the plains.

Jimmy Carter became president down in the States and the first thing he did was pardon the draft dodgers. You can come home, he said.

My father couldn't. His father had closed the door, hard and fast. My grandmother tried once, secretly, to whisper through to her son and grandson, to the girls she would've happily claimed as daughter and granddaughter. But the old man, a twice-wounded World War II veteran, proud, heaved his weight against that door. It stayed closed.

They lived in Minnesota. Detroit was almost a thousand miles away, and we went there. Dad went to school, became a nurse. My mother worked in bookstores, wrote and read her poems in coffeehouses. She took her turn at school, studied chemistry. She's never considered herself a scientist, though, always a poet. Over the years her poems became longer, monologues. Her monologues became flamboyant, performance.

Soon, Detroit was too crowded for them. We moved to Montana, where it was easier to breathe in the mountains.

Then, Colorado. Then, New Mexico. Now, Minnesota.

He hasn't been back in twenty years. Not even for his mother's funeral four years ago, or for his father's last summer. His old man died without a will so everything went to my dad and his brother. Maybe it was my grandfather's way of saying, Come back.

Or, maybe, bad financial planning.

Either way, my dad now owns a fully furnished house in Red Cedar, Minnesota. And after years of dragging me around — two countries, six states, seven cities, and how many schools? — he's been inspired to hold me prisoner and force-feed a hometown.

Haircut —

By noon most everyone had migrated to the indoor pool. The water and lounge chairs were filled with bodies. Toneless wrinkled flesh, no shame.

Border sat on a stool in the middle of the lobby while the man with the thin mustache worked on his hair.

CNN droned on: "Border tension remains high . . ."

Snip. Snip. Snip.

"Buzz the rest, please," Border said to his personal barber. "Make it just like his," and he pointed to Colonel John Farmer, retired.

Border's father watched with a few others as his son's hair fell onto the floor. He tugged on his gray ponytail. Mystified.

The Story, II —

My name, that's a story right there. And it's one I've heard often enough.

No one knew what my father was going to do when he ran, back in '70. He was alone and scared. He was breaking the law, breaking hearts.

"But the minute I crossed the border," he always says when he tells the story, "I was safe and happy and certain I'd done the right thing. Just how I felt when I first held you."

Sweet, Dad. Sweet.

Might have been worse, though. He could have named me for the border crossing, for the first solid ground of Canada. Might have called me, oh . . . Pigeon River.

Mozart and Midnight Oil —

The barber refused money. "Happy to do it," he said. "I wasn't going anywhere." He flipped a hand at the lobby window. Snow fell relentlessly.

Still, it wasn't blowing so much, and a large group decided to walk three blocks to a restaurant. Everyone was tired of donuts. Border's father went along and brought back three grilled cheese sandwiches for his son.

Border took the sandwiches to their room. While he ate he decided to call his mother. Time to check in, but where would she be? At work or in jail?

17

"She's home sick," said her lab assistant.

"Not in jail?"

"I guess she never made it to the protest. She woke up that morning with a raging fever and a terrible sore throat."

"There's a virus stronger than her convictions?"

"Don't say that to her," the assistant cautioned.

He decided against calling her at home. She'd be bummed about missing the protest and, besides, she got really grumpy when sick.

Border watched television, then fell asleep. He woke up hungry and left the room to find food. Bagels and juice would do.

Late afternoon — no one in the pool, but the lobby was crowded. Right away Border could tell that people were tired of each other.

News from the Gulf didn't help. People argued — men with men, women with women, Border noticed, wondering about that. Colonel John Farmer was especially angry.

"No guns for oil," he said.

Border grinned. He'd heard that often enough. "Don't you think we should start a war with Saddam?"

Lil smiled.

John scowled. "I'm a soldier, Border, and a soldier obeys his commander. If our country goes to war, I will support it. And you have to admit, Saddam is one crazy tyrant. If we don't stop him . . ." He shook his head. "It was so clear, so *clear,* back in forty-one."

When the arguing threatened to get personal, Border slipped away to his room and returned with his recorder. He started playing softly in the corner by the coffee pot. At first only Lil listened, but as soon as John Farmer heard the music he bellowed a command for silence, and Border had everyone's attention.

He played beautifully, he always did. Practically a prodigy, he thought as his fingers tapped along the sleek wooden stem.

The crowd favorite was "Red Sails in the Sunset" — his Midnight Oil medley, not the old ballad, though he played that too. Then he played his own Mozart arrangements, wishing all the while he dared put out his hat for contributions. A crowd like this would be good for forty, fifty bucks. Better than a crowd of tourists in Old Town.

His hat. He stopped midnote.

Riley also had his hat.

The Story, III —

There's more, of course. There are the years of silence between my father and his parents, years of moving, different schools, new apartments, countless strangers who became family friends, political protests and political performances. Lots of cats.

Dana and I grew.

Mom and Dad grew apart. Isn't that what's always said? But that's their story. I don't know it. I can only imagine.

Another Departure —

In the morning Border carried John and Lil's suitcases to their car. The snow had stopped and the plows were out. John was confident the roads would be clear enough, headed south and west.

"They'll be worse going your way," he cautioned. "You're chasing the storm."

Border nodded. How true.

Others were leaving and good-byes were said, and the parking lot was as cheery and loud as the lobby had been the previous day. Border was hugged several times.

Twice by John, who said, as he pulled away from the first hug, "Your father is a brave fool. I grew up in a town like his hometown. I know how those places are. We're about to get our butts kicked into a war and that's a crazy time for a draft dodger to go back home. Crazy. Every loudmouthed, know-it-all patriot will be after his balls."

"Farmer, stop," said his wife.

Border's eyes widened. "He told you?"

"He and I had lunch together yesterday," John said. "It's a talent of mine, getting people to talk. Though it appears I needed a bit more time to work on you."

Lil opened a portfolio and handed Border a drawing. The paper was white and it caught the sun, and he was blinded until he shielded his eyes.

"Pencil isn't my favorite medium," she said, "but it was all I had at hand."

Border and Recorder, she had written on the top of the sheet. And that's what it was, a picture of him playing.

"Please send it to your mother," Lil said.

"She might like to see the haircut," added John, then he moved in for the second hug.

Border waved as they drove away, and just before he turned to go back into the motel, he saw a car window roll down.

"One more thing," John called. "Take your father to a barber."

Border saluted.

20

Lil accelerated, snow shot out from under car tires, and their long, black Buick joined the procession of huge American cars leaving the motel parking lot, southbound.

Another Haircut —

Traveling in the wake of the blizzard, Border marveled at its power. Starting somewhere in New Mexico, it had blown across Texas and Oklahoma, caught them in Missouri, then surged ahead up into Iowa.

The whiteness was vast, though not exactly flat, the way he'd expected, because the snow had drifted and duned.

Border drove after Des Moines, and while keeping his eyes on the road ahead, he thought back to home. Wondered what Riley and the others were doing. Wondered about the burnt kid. Wondered if Weber would go ahead and pierce his tongue. If Celeste would contact the baby's father. If Riley had sold his hat.

Border ran his palm over his buzzed head. Would the hat fit now?

He exited at Mason City, the sign said, and turned west to Clear Lake, the sign said. His father said, "Hey?"

Border didn't speak until they found a downtown. He parked, looked the stores over, then pointed. "Your turn to get a haircut."

"Hey?" his father said again.

"John Farmer might be right, about being an easy target."

While his father got cut and shaved, Border sat in a chair and paged through a *Playboy*, wondering.

He listened to his father joke and trade stories with the barber. Two men with time on their hands came into the shop and joined the conversation.

Hospital stories. Border had heard most of them, so he listened mostly to the sound of the voices, to the odd little noises the men made while listening to his father. Over the edge of the magazine he observed the looks they exchanged, the smiles they bestowed on the stranger.

When they left he knew that the barbershop men would feel they'd had a good afternoon, and would tell others about this dang man who came in, a nurse wouldja believe?

Border, in the car, listened as his father shouted good-bye to the men, and, funny, just then it felt okay to be his kid.

II

Arrival

Hometown —

"It's an ugly town, Dad."

"Nothing's changed," his father whispered.

"Then it's always been ugly?"

No answer.

"I realize most towns are ugly from the highway, but this seems especially bad. It's so flat."

"Welcome to Minnesota, Border."

"Aren't there supposed to be lakes? Isn't there *anything* to look at? Oops, there's a mall."

His father turned to look. "That's new."

Five more minutes to the exit, a few more while they drove down streets lined with small houses, and his father must have said "Nothing's changed" twenty times. Border was tempted to scream at him to quit, but he let him have his time of wonder.

The chant changed. "That's it. That's it. That's it," the old man said, pointing to a blue house.

"Welcome home, Dad."

Border carried bags into the house. He kicked off his shoes and wandered through the rooms. The neatness tickled him. Of course, no one had been living here since his grandfather's death. And his uncle had taken some things, he knew, and the clothing had gone to Goodwill, and there'd been a cleaning lady. All these details had been discussed in long conversations between his father and uncle, who lived in Chicago.

"You want the big bedroom?" Border asked.

"Of course."

Border chose a room for himself. He supposed it had been his father's. Twin beds, two dressers. Spruce green covers on the bed, matching curtains.

No posters or pictures. He didn't know why he expected some. It had been twenty years since a child had lived there, and the last one, his father, had been wiped from the family's record as if he'd never been alive.

Border had never lived in a house before. Always it had been apartments, some so large that there were hidden rooms, some so small he couldn't step out of bed without being in the kitchen or the bathroom or — the worst — his parents' bedroom. This house wasn't big, but there were lots of rooms. He found a workshop and a sewing room. Two bathrooms. Three televisions. He opened a door and discovered a washer and dryer. He smiled. No more trips to the laundromat.

"We'll need food," he said to his father when they met in the kitchen. His father nodded, then sat down and looked around the room.

"Seems pretty weird, I suppose," Border said. "To be here and all."

His father nodded again, then closed his eyes and rubbed his forehead.

Border shrugged. He put on his jacket and went to the garage. The walks and driveway were loaded with snow. He

26

foraged in the garage, found a shovel, and started clearing the driveway.

He had never shoveled snow before. As apartment dwellers, they'd always left it to the landlord. It was strangely satisfying work. Every few feet he paused and admired what he'd accomplished. He was leaning against the long-handled shovel, surveying the length of black driveway he'd exposed, when a garage door immediately across the street started rising slowly. Before it had risen to its full height a car backed out, just slipping through the opening.

It was a copper-colored Cadillac convertible, with a raised black top. The driver honked twice, then accelerated and backed straight across the street onto Border's driveway. The car stopped a few inches from the garage door.

The driver stepped out. It was a lady, and Border saw right away she had copper-colored hair. She matched her Cadillac.

Staredown. Border refused to speak, and he saw that the lady couldn't. His dad came out of the house then, and she ran forward, hugged him, then waved hands in front of her tear-streaked face.

"Too much," she said finally. "It's all too much. How long has it been, Gumbo?"

Border smiled at hearing his father's childhood nickname. *You're home now, Dad,* he thought.

"Hello, Connie," the old man said.

He should have known; he could have guessed. Connie. The mother of his father's oldest friend, the woman who always kept track of where they were living and what they were doing and never failed to send at least a Christmas letter full of news from the old hometown.

"Wave to Paul," she commanded. "He's sitting by the window. He had his bypass surgery two weeks ago and he's not moving much yet."

They dutifully waved to the unseen husband.

"Border, baby."

He cringed and braced himself for a hug.

It was a good one, a real lung crusher. When she pulled back she inhaled and spoke at the same time. "I can't believe it. Gumbo's boy." Exhaled. Her eyes widened, smile broadened. "Border, sweetheart, I just have to tell you I saw your mother perform."

People always had to tell him that.

"She came to Minneapolis, you know, right before Thanksgiving. The kids came down from up north and we met in Minneapolis and saw the show." She pressed two fingers against her lips and inhaled. A ghost cigarette.

"I've wondered a few times since," and her smile turned wicked, "if her show had anything to do with Paul's heart failure!"

"We're unpacking, Connie," Border's father said wearily. "Tomorrow I start work."

"I know you do. The hospital called me because they wanted to know if you were here yet. They hadn't heard. Lots of people have called, Gumbo. There's plenty of folks who want to see you — you'd be surprised how many are still here from your class. And your wife even called. Twice."

"She's not my wife, Connie. Not for a year now."

"I know that, but let me say, we had a *very* interesting conversation. Let's go in and have some coffee and I'll tell you."

"The cupboards are bare."

"They are not. I brought a few things over on Monday. I

28

have a key, you know. I've had it for thirty years, boys, I've never hesitated to use it, and I don't see the reason to change. C'mon Gumbo, let's make coffee, and we can talk."

Border didn't want coffee and didn't want to talk. He stayed outside, leaning against the shovel and looking at the street. Four blocks of nearly identical houses, each with a tidy, snow-covered yard. His was punctuated in the center by a single tree. Snow around it was unmarked, pristine. Perfect for snow angels. He dropped the shovel and stepped into the snow. The crust held him for a moment, then gave way on his third step and he tumbled forward. He felt the cold snow slide into his shoes and shoot up his wrists. A passing car loaded with kids honked. He could see the driver peering, the riders pointing and laughing.

Border scooped up snow and formed a ball to fling at the car. Childish, but satisfying.

When it smacked the taillight, the car slowed, the window reeled down, and curses were hurled. Then it gunned and sped away. Border felt stupidly pleased.

Shopping —

Border followed Connie around the grocery store. She had insisted on taking him shopping while his father unpacked. Only it was pretty clear she had no interest in groceries. She was too busy talking — to the deli workers, the cart collectors, every third person in the aisles. While she chatted and laughed, he selected food from the shelves and put it in the cart.

When he was introduced to someone, he'd nod and then

stand still while the person studied his face, his clothes, his height. Border on display, just like a sale rack of cookies.

". . . Gumbo Baker's boy. They've come to live in town, you know," he heard Connie say every five minutes. Then a fresh inspection began. He was civil. Some people harrumphed and turned away, some hugged his shoulders. One lady, who seemed to be a particular friend of Connie's, clapped her hands on her rosy cheeks and shook her head. "I knew your grandma so well," she said, and Border wished he'd paid attention to her name. "She put up with so much crap from your grandpa, and it just killed her to have her boy living so far away. We offered — didn't we, Cons? — we offered to drive her to Canada to see your dad, but she was the good wife, always the good wife, your grandma, in spite of all the BS she took from him. She was just paralyzed, wasn't she, Cons?"

Connie nodded.

"Oh, those were wicked times."

Border set some salsa in the cart. So he had a family with a past. Well, he'd always known that, but all these people in this grocery store seemed to know a lot more about it than he did.

The strange lady with red hair (Border wondered about the color of her car) got a little choked up. "Gol darn it," she said, "if she weren't dead already, why it would just kill her to see you, all big like this, and those years you were little just gone and lost."

Lord, tears. And these were worse, coming from a stranger. Border reached for soup cans, two for $1.99, but he didn't make it; instead, smack in the center of aisle five, he got hugged hard by a nice-smelling, red-haired lady.

A Boy and His Car —

It didn't take long to settle in because they hadn't brought many belongings. After all, the house was fully furnished. It even came with a late-model Oldsmobile in the garage.

"You love the Volvo, so will this car be mine?" Border asked, hopeful. He pictured himself driving the Olds with a load of friends along, cruising down Central in Albuquerque, or heading out to the hills. A road trip to the Grand Canyon. Who wants to go? Hop in!

He frowned. They'd need a special seat for Celeste's baby.

Border ran his hand over the hood, over the gleaming maroon surface.

Of course! He would do what Connie did: He'd color his hair to match his car. Perfect.

"*Your* car?" his father said. "Are you crazy?"

First Night —

Border was in bed by ten — nothing else to do — but he didn't sleep because his father was making too much noise prowling around the house. Around eleven he heard him talking on the phone.

"It's all so weird, Jeff. You warned me . . ."

Border sighed and rolled over so that he could look out a window. When his father got talking to his old friend Jeff, Connie's kid, sometimes they didn't let go for an hour. He wondered if he'd have an old friend to call when he was pushing forty. Doubted it. What with all the moving around, the closest he'd ever come to having a best friend was this

31

past year in Albuquerque, when he met Riley and the others. He couldn't imagine calling any of them when he needed to talk. Hard to reach any of them by phone, of course. And then it had always seemed to work the other way; they called him.

Border, I'm at the shelter, it's a bad scene, come get me.

I'm in labor, Border, and my mother's too drunk to drive me to the hospital.

Would you loan me ten bucks?

He could call Dana. Awful, really, to think that he'd turn forty someday, and his sister would be his one friend. His sister.

His father finished talking on the phone and, cheered, whistled as he closed down the house for the night. He paused at Border's door, knocked, and peeked in.

"You aren't really asleep, right?"

"Not now."

"I'm feeling okay about this. Are you feeling okay?"

Dad, puh-leez. "Can I answer that later?"

"Good night, Border."

Border burrowed into the bedding. Okay with *this*? With bedtime at ten, spruce green curtains, Minnesota?

Puh-leez.

First Day –

His father took the Olds to work.

"Wait," Border said, before he backed out of the garage. And he ran inside, found the camera, and returned to the garage to take a picture. "Mom should see this," he said as he snapped. "You in a big new car." His father didn't think it was funny and made a face in time to be recorded by the camera.

"Good luck," Border said.

"Go to school," his father replied.

Border went out for breakfast. Trying to remember the route he'd taken with Connie, he drove around town for half an hour, looking for the grocery store because he remembered it had a coffee shop. He didn't find it, which was no easy trick; it was a small town.

He did find the main street, and there was a restaurant across from the courthouse.

Border walked in and people looked up. He sat in a booth, greeted the waitress, and ordered eggs.

Two old men wearing denim jackets and caps swiveled around on their counter stools. Red Cap spoke. "Skipping school?" They laughed, the waitress too.

"Eating breakfast," he answered.

"Eating breakfast, then skipping school?"

A cop walked into the café, slung his jacket on a hook, took command of a stool. The old men greeted him and both pointed at Border.

"Got a truant for you," said Blue Cap.

Cop raised an eyebrow.

Border, picturing a police escort to school for his first appearance, thought fast. "Doctor's appointment."

Cop lost interest, turned to the coffee the waitress was pouring for him.

"Something serious?" asked Red Cap, looking concerned.

Border thought of make-believe, shut-you-up answers: AIDS, cancer, girlfriend's obstetrician. "Dermatologist," he said.

The old men and the waitress talked then about their

33

grandchildren, and the flaws they possessed — mostly bad complexions and bad driving records.

Border didn't hide that he was listening. "I've never had an accident," he said. "Unless you count the time I hit a pigeon."

Ha, ha, they liked that.

"So long, big fella," the waitress said when he paid his check. "And they've got real good stuff for your problem now. Just you see."

Good stuff for his problem? Like an Oldsmobile, a gas credit card, a clear road to the Southwest?

He found the high school and drove around it twice, thinking, *This is it, the scene of my new life.* It was an old building, three stories of red brick spread over two blocks. Pausing at a stop sign, he glanced up and saw a boy looking out a school window. The boy spotted Border, waved, then pressed his body against the glass, arms spread, mouth open.

"Let me out of here!" Border shouted for him.

Chicken, Dad —

He spent the afternoon at home fixing a big meal for supper. His dad's first day at work; the old man should be rewarded. He made cookies, he roasted chicken, he mashed potatoes, he tossed a salad.

His father was late. Border ate alone.

When he did arrive, his father was apologetic. "I didn't know you'd do this. It was hard to get away."

"How did it go? Did anyone remember Gumbo the draft dodger? Did they give you trouble?"

"They gave me a cake. It had red roses and 'Welcome

Home' on it. I knew three of the nurses and the x-ray tech from high school. They've never left town. Amazing."

"No trouble at all?"

His father shook his head slowly. "It was a great day, Border. How was yours? How was school?"

"I went *to* the school."

"What?"

"I drove around a few times, then came home. Don't be so glum. I wanted to make a good supper for you. That takes time."

The old man's great day was over. He sat wearily in a kitchen chair, alternately looking at his son and the television. A reporter in Saudi Arabia had surrounded herself with eager and happy soldiers, all of them waiting to take on Saddam Hussein.

"I am just so proud," one shouted into the reporter's microphone, "to be an American soldier."

"Turn it off and eat, Dad," Border said. "Have some —"

Oops.

His father looked at the leftovers on the table, then looked at his son. A smile returned to his face. "Some *what*, Border?"

The small kitchen was filled with TV noise, with the whooping and cheering of American soldiers five thousand miles from home, proud and ready to fight a war.

"Chicken."

Time Runs Out —

Border procrastinated. He stalled. He faked sick. He did everything he could think of to avoid going to school. He had to, because whenever he thought of walking into a classroom for the first time, his stomach roiled, his head reeled, and he wished himself dead.

His father allowed this. Bent over backward to be sympathetic and understanding. "When you're ready," he said. Border recognized guilt, and he let it simmer.

Paul and Connie came for supper one night. They drove over, backing up to the garage. Border cooked pollo en adobo, and Paul watched the final preparations, nodding approvingly when he let loose with the chilis.

The food was good, and it was impossible not to laugh with Connie around. Paul and the old man wanted to watch news. The deadline for the UN's ultimatum to Iraq was approaching. Connie would have none of it. "The last war took enough out of me," she said. "I'll have nothing to do with this one."

Her oldest son had died in Vietnam, a Marine. Border wanted to know what she thought of his father, the draft dodger. He swallowed the question. He'd ask another time.

Paul pushed back from the table. "Gumbo," he said, and Border saw his father wince; the old nickname grated. "If Border were my son, tomorrow morning I'd grab him by the neck and march him to the high school."

Border looked around, saw Connie nodding, saw his father blush, saw Paul reach for more rice. He knew then he'd be back in school tomorrow.

"That's the last time I cook for you, Paul," he said.

"Then we'll eat at my house," Paul answered. "Sunday?"

Border shook hands with the guidance counselor, who was gung ho. A grinning boy came up to him. "I'll be your guide," he said. "I'm a sophomore, too. We have homeroom and two classes together. Do you play hockey? Football? With your size, you'd be great."

Border thought, *You're why I hate high school.* He spoke, "I play recorder."

The boy smiled. "Cool," he said.

Homeroom hell. Thirty faces looked up, thirty minds came to conclusions. Thirty-one: Border decided he hated them all. While the teacher checked over the papers Border handed her, he looked out the window. Snowy yards, slushy streets, big American cars crawling toward the small downtown.

Border closed his eyes and was on the campus at UNM, playing for money while Riley and Weber and the others joked, tossed a ball, and Celeste fed her baby.

He took a seat and stretched his legs. He rubbed a hand over the sandpaper-roughness of his pimpled face. He pretended no one was looking.

"Border Baker, welcome to Red Cedar High School," the teacher chirped.

She was young and eager. Border didn't smile.

She said, "Tell us something about yourself!"

Border stiffened. Felt his neck go red, felt his zits bulge. But he sensed he could sit silently forever, and she'd wait. So he spoke: "I don't want to be here."

She was shocked, she was speechless. Not the students. No — they roared, they clapped, they shouted and stamped. Border, surprised, smiled and looked around while his fingers tapped frantically on his thighs.

First hour was a mental muddle. Second hour a blurry nightmare. Third hour Border got hungry, realized then that he'd forgotten to pack a lunch and neglected to take lunch money. By fourth hour he was gnawing on pencils — nervous work for his jaws. A boy noticed and called him Woodchuck; then others picked it up and by seventh period he couldn't walk down the hall without some guy dipping his head in greeting and saying, "Hey, Chuck."

"Day one, and I survived," he said to himself as he made a fast, head-down exit to his car the instant the final bell rang. "I'll have to tell my mother."

And he did. Went straight home, wolfed down a snack, and called his mother. Not that he expected her to be home. Two-thirty in Santa Fe, she'd be at the lab — his favorite time to call. He liked talking to her machine. It never asked questions.

Message —

Okay, here's an update. You will be glad to know I finally went to school. It was pretty special. Did you love high school? You've never told me. I bet you didn't. I bet most people don't, which makes me wonder why adults get thoroughly freaked when their kids don't like it. But maybe you did. Maybe you were just the most popular kid in school and you never told us. Were you ever prom queen, or anything? Is that a secret you don't want your kids to know? C'mon, Mom, tell me.

Heard from Dana? Tell the rat to call.

It's snowing again and it's cold. Thought you'd want to know.

Day two didn't go any better, though he remembered to bring a lunch. A hometown hero was visiting and there was a special assembly. The hero was introduced as a brilliant student, Red Cedar's best ever, with a track record that included Yale, Cambridge, and Columbia. Now he was a top aide to some state department honcho. But not too important to come back for his grandmother's funeral and talk to the kids at his old high school.

"George Bush is the greatest leader in the world!" the hero crowed. "And watch out, Saddam — we are going to kick your Iraqi butt!"

While the auditorium erupted, Border sat quietly, wondering about the value of an expensive education.

They had a pop quiz in history. Border stared at the sheet of questions a full minute before raising his hand.

"Hmm, yes, New Boy?" the teacher said, frowning.

"I just got here, sir, and my old school was covering different stuff."

"Hmm, try your best."

He blew it. He confused the Preamble of the Constitution with the Declaration of Independence. Ten points. He couldn't identify names on a list, couldn't tell who was a general or who was a delegate to the Constitutional Convention or who was an explorer. Another ten. He thought the Articles of Confederation had something to do with the Civil War. The Confederacy, right? Six points.

It added up to a big fat *F.*

That was all he was seeing and thinking about when he left history. Which was why he didn't see the boy lurking by his locker, why he was surprised when suddenly there were hands on his shoulders and he was slammed against the gray steel door.

The big fat *F* in Border's eyes dissolved into the boy's face.

"Yeah?" said Border.

"Your dad's the draft dodger, right?"

"You got a name?"

"My name, you stinking son of a worthless traitor, is Bryan. Welcome to Red Cedar. My uncle used to be in school with your dad, and you know what he says? He says your dad fried his brains with drugs. Says he was called Gumbo because that's what his mind was like, after all the stuff he did. He says your dad oughta be forgiven for running from the draft 'cuz he was so drug-soaked, he didn't know what he was doing."

"He knew."

"That's what I think. I also think that when we start dropping bombs on Saddam, you know what we oughta send along?"

"Tell me, Bryan."

"The brainless, gutless body of every draft-dodging cow-ardly traitor."

"You want to talk brains, Bryan?" Border said cheerfully. "Well, I bet yours wouldn't fill a nut cup."

Border moved first, so Bryan's fist and knee collided with the locker.

Message, II —

Hello, all you residents of 1010 Baldwin. Residents and drift-ers, lovers and friends. I suppose there are a few of all those hanging around. So what else is new? Whoever gets to this first, please tell my mother that her son got clobbered in school today. Cool, huh? This beefy gorilla just had to tell me what he thought about my father the draft dodger. I suspect this is not the first time a student in an American school has had a violent encounter with a steel locker. Maybe they should make those things out of something else. I'm fine. But I thought you might want to know, Mom. Maybe put it in a show. Get to the heart of it when you're on stage. I even have a title for you: *Sins of the Father*. Of course, you'd have to do a little cross-dressing, but you've done that. Like the show where you played me. Remember? The show where you had the audience rolling on the floor as you re-enacted my only attempt at athletics? The show where you got up in front of people night after night and talked about your son, the hopeful little leaguer who stopped a line drive with his unprotected nuts. What did you call that show? Oh, yeah, I remember: *Private Parts*.

Choices —

The off-the-hook signal beeped in his ear and Border hung up the phone, glad he hadn't actually dialed. Soon after the separation he'd figured out that it wasn't smart to leave really disturbing messages. She panicked easily: Come for the weekend! We have to talk! His personal rule for family communication: Limit the bad news, limit the sarcasm. Keep it sweet, keep 'em happy, keep 'em quiet.

He checked the clock and frowned. An hour to suppertime and it was his turn to cook. That's how they did things. Any other way would be oppressive. His parents hated oppression, especially in a family. So they took turns. Cooking, shopping, taking out garbage, cleaning, school conferences — no, not that; they usually went together, even when they were no longer living together.

Border suspected they had taken turns with love affairs, but he wasn't sure. It wasn't talked about, and not all the family's private parts turned up in his mother's shows.

He checked the fridge for leftovers. "Bless ya Dad," he said, spotting the cold pot roast. His father believed in taking turns, but he was realistic; his turn, he always made too much.

Border sat at the kitchen table with cookies and milk, thinking back to the days when they didn't have cookies and milk. No sweets, back then, and for a year or so, they were lactose-free. That was in Fort Collins, between Missoula and Albuquerque. Part of fourth, all of fifth, part of sixth grade. That's how he remembered the places they'd lived: by the grades he was in.

He hummed his father's favorite, John Lennon: ". . . places I remember . . ." Fingers tapped. Playing the Beatles was always good for huge money. On the plaza in Old Town, he'd rip off a few Beatles' songs, the sweet ballads, and the baby boomers would go wild. Pats on the head, bills in the hat. Whatta kick, they'd say, to see such a punk playing the Beatles. Isn't he a sweet boy? Those days, if he could stomach an afternoon of Lennon and McCartney, Border would go home with near a hundred bucks.

He turned on the TV. War news. No, prewar news. Today was it, the ultimatum deadline, and Saddam hadn't pulled out of Kuwait. The reporter was interviewing an American general, who stared sternly at the camera and said something belligerent about needing the support of the American people. Border cringed, expecting the general to reach out of the TV and slam him against the wall.

You son-of-a-traitor.

"I am not," Border shouted. "I'm the son of a . . . of a nurse!"

"Who you shouting at, honey?"

Border twisted in his chair, just as Connie walked into the kitchen. She tossed her keys and purse onto the counter and pulled open the refrigerator door. "You boys got any of that funny-flavored water?"

"Did you knock?"

"No. Should I? I will if you want me to. Paul says I should. He's usually right. Who were you yelling at?"

"TV."

"That's useless."

"Feels good."

"So do a lot of things, hon, but that doesn't mean it's smart to do them. How was school?"

Border hit the off button on the remote. "I got jumped."

She pulled out a chair and sat. "What?"

"This guy called me the worthless son of a traitor, or maybe it was the son of a worthless traitor. The son of something. We had an assembly and it was pretty much a war rally. He was pumped up and I was in his way."

"Are you hurt?"

"No."

"Did you tell the principal?"

Border rolled his eyes.

"I think you should, hon. She's a sharp gal. I play bridge with her at the club. She'd do something. I think —"

"Connie, have you ever been the new kid in school? Have you even been in a high school lately? I am not whining to the principal. And don't you dare tell her. Or Dad. Sorry I even mentioned anything. Dead issue. What are you up to?"

She thought a bit before answering, not wanting to change the subject. Then she sighed and shrugged. "Paul told me to get out of his way. He's working and I'm a distraction."

"That's good that he's writing again." Both Connie and Paul had worked for forty years at the local meat-packing plant, Porter's Pork. Three months into retirement, Paul had gotten restless and gotten inspired. He started writing a novel, a murder mystery.

Five years and four mysteries later, Paul Sanborn was a well-known author. There'd even been an article on his books in *People* magazine, one that included a photo of him standing in front of a life-sized illustration of his detective-heroine — Rosie Sticker, a lady golf pro at a country club.

"He's driving me crazy. If he gets started on this new book, we won't be going anywhere this winter."

"You weren't going anywhere anyway. He's sick."

"I figured in four, five weeks, we could take off for some place warm. He'd be well enough then."

"You should buy him one of those portable computers, those notebook things."

"What do they do?"

"They're small and they work on a battery. They go anywhere. He could sit in the Cadillac and write while you drive."

Connie stood up. "Let's go to Rochester. Think they sell them there?"

"Probably. Of course, they cost a few thousand."

"Rosie Sticker will pay. Let's go."

Homework . . . or a ride in the Cadillac.

Didn't need to flip a coin to make that decision.

He left a note: *Leftovers in fridge. I've run off with Connie.*

Road Trip —

Connie drove fast. Border wasn't surprised. She drove fast and she talked — about her long-gone first husband, about Paul, his new book, the women at the club where she played cards, her son and his family, about the impending war.

"Everybody thinks this war with Iraq," she said, "will be a friggin' picnic. Don't they know that war means dead children? And for what? Oil?"

What would John Farmer say? "Saddam's kind of a tyrannical bastard, Connie. World War Two happened because no one stopped Hitler, right?"

"Listen to you! Funny, you don't look like a Republican. Isn't that the way, though: Kids always gotta do what drives their parents crazy."

"Maybe I believe it."

Connie's voice was low and raspy, scratched raw from years of cigarette smoking. She had stopped when Paul first had signs of heart trouble, but the damage was done. Her voice sounded like the idling engine of a snowplow.

And it rolled out, laughing. "Maybe you do. Oh, honey, maybe you do."

He wanted to ask her about the son that died. He knew the name — Tommy — but not much more. Do you ask people, he wondered, about their dead kids?

45

The lady was a mind reader. "Now my son Tommy," she said, "didn't believe in much at all. Well, maybe he believed in a good party. I passed that much on to him, I guess. But he did what he had to do. He was a Marine, and Marines go to war. His country said fight, so he fought."

"Not my dad."

"That's true enough. He did exactly what he wasn't supposed to do."

"He ran." Something he hasn't given up. Toronto, Winnipeg, Detroit, Missoula . . .

She shook her head. "Sweet old Gumbo, a draft dodger. Oh, how that shook us all up, I tell you."

"Weren't you mad at him, Connie? I mean, after all, your son died in the war."

"Border, for thirty years I lived across the street from your grandparents. And while the kids were growing up, it was like it didn't matter which house they slept in. Some days would go by and I swear I'd see more of your dad than my own kids, especially if your grandpa was in one of his moods. Lord knows I fed them all often enough. Then those little boys grew up. Tommy was killed. Jeff and your uncle managed to escape the draft, but not Gumbo. They called his number, and he couldn't face it, so he ran. Oh, I was worried for him, but I wasn't mad, Border. It was a war you couldn't believe in; one boy dying was enough."

She pressed two fingers to her lips and inhaled, breathing in a ghost.

Connie quit talking and played music. The Cadillac had a good sound system and she had a library of tapes. "Enough to get us to Florida and back without repeating a single one," she told him. She popped in Aretha Franklin and let it blast.

"Maudie bought me this," she shouted over the music. Maud was her son's wife. "She and I took a trip to the Ozarks last summer, just the two of us, and she didn't like any of my tapes, so she made me stop in Kansas City to buy something she did like. Now I think it's my favorite."

Border leaned his head against the leather seat and let his fingers tap while Connie sang along with the Queen of Soul.

He thought about how every child has four grandparents. Odds were a kid would know at least one. He hadn't. All four dead. Two before he was even born, the other two before they'd admit him into their lives. He closed his eyes and conjured up grandparents. What would they be like? Maybe one would look a little like Colonel John Farmer. Maybe one was an artist. Maybe one . . .

Stupid. His family was his family. What they were, that's all he had.

He opened his eyes and saw that it was snowing. Connie drove on, oblivious, doing eighty. He shifted in his seat, and she turned her head, caught his eye, and winked.

Driving in the Car with Connie —

The computer salesman couldn't believe his luck. Connie took five minutes to find what she wanted, another five to be persuaded to buy an armload of accessories, five more to pay. In under twenty minutes, she was back in the car with a four-thousand-dollar surprise for her husband.

"Hope he likes it," Border said.

"He'd better. I'll give it to him tonight, but I'll call it a birthday present. His birthday is in two weeks. Now I don't

47

have to get him that rototiller. Oh my gosh, look at this snow. When did this start?"

"On the way here. You didn't notice?"

"You had me thinking too hard, hon. Rats. I thought maybe we could stop somewhere for a nice steak. It's not much of a town, but they do have some decent restaurants that know how to grill a chunk of beef."

"Maybe we should head home. Dad might be worried. And Paul might want to use his new toy."

She paused before inserting the ignition key. "I might be wrong about this. He might never get out of that chair now. Just sit in the recliner in his pajamas with this machine on his lap and crank out his sexy mysteries."

"Are they sexy?"

"You haven't read one of Paul's books?"

"I don't really like mysteries."

"I'll tell you the truth, Border. I've only read one. Part of one, really. When I came across the very first bedroom scene, I said to myself, I don't want to know this. Don't want to know what my husband is about to tell the world."

He couldn't quite imagine her caring and was about to say so, but she pulled the mind-reading trick again.

"I don't talk about *everything*."

She didn't talk at all on the way back to Red Cedar. Border felt chatty, and it seemed like a good chance to hear about his dad's family and childhood, but he was good at reading adult signals, so he kept his mouth closed. Another time.

Border hummed a tune, an original, tapping it out. Da-da-da-da-da-da-DE-da.

Driving in the car with KA-nee.

Better than playing pyroball.

Bombs Away —

On the fridge, a note for Border: *Paul made chili. I'm at his house. The war has started and we are watching. You are welcome. Your mother called twice, you might want to call her. Dana has disappeared.*

III

War

Missing —

Border was hungry, but he wanted information. He called his mother, got her machine.

Hi, this is Diana. Please leave a message, especially if you are my daughter. Is this a joke, Dana? Where are you? I'm at Lee's. Call me there.

Lee was the new lover, not a favorite of Border or Dana. He wouldn't call her there; doubted if Dana would. He left a message: She'll turn up, Mom.

Would she?

"Do you know anything, Dad? What did Mom tell you?" he asked as soon as he walked into Connie and Paul's living room. The men had finished eating, but Connie was just sitting down to a bowl of chili. Paul was examining the new computer. Border tossed his jacket onto a chair.

His father shrugged. "Not much. Her grandparents put her on the plane in South Carolina, she had to switch in Atlanta, and she didn't get off in Albuquerque."

"So she's in Atlanta," Border said.

"I refuse to be worried," said his father.

"Gumbo!" said Connie.

Paul tapped at the computer on his lap.

"Maybe he's right," said Border. "My sister is smart; no one could hurt her." He sat next to his father on the sofa. "She bites."

Connie made a face. "Don't joke. Do you really think she just took off because she didn't want to go home?"

Border and his father exchanged looks, then both smiled. "Yes," said Border.

Connie sighed. "Then I won't worry, either." She sank back in her chair.

"Chili's in the kitchen," said Paul. "Help yourself." He didn't look up. Tap tap, tap tap.

Watching the War —

The chili was good and Border had seconds. Just as he was refilling his bowl, he heard his father swear, then moan. *Must be the president*, thought Border, *or he's thinking of Dana.* He turned around to look at the TV screen through the kitchen doorway and sure enough there was George Bush, his somber face filling the screen.

The president looked straight at the camera, at the American people, and made promises that first night of war. He said the liberation of Kuwait would not be another Vietnam, and Border's father groaned. He said he had not, would not, tie the hands of the military leadership in carrying out the war. He said he thought it would not last long, nor would there be many casualties.

"American," said Border's father. "He means American casualties."

He and Connie began a gentle argument, but Border didn't

pay attention because the war was more interesting. CNN had reporters in Baghdad, where the missiles were hitting. The target area, all the grim analysts and generals on the screen called it.

One reporter, trapped in Baghdad, called it something else: the center of hell.

Paul, too, was more interested in what was on TV than in arguing, though he wasn't so mesmerized that he stopped typing on the new computer.

"Huh!" Connie said and rose from her chair. "I've heard enough from you, Gumbo. Who needs a drink?"

"I do," said Border. "Scotch and soda." He was ignored.

"One more thing," said his father, "just one more thing, Connie."

"What?" she snarled. Border frowned — not so gentle an argument, after all. "Are you going to tell me Hussein isn't evil? Are you going to tell me that the whole United Nations is wrong? Bloody hell, Gumbo, never before, not once, have the countries on this planet been so unified. That's wrong? Are you going to say that?"

"I'm going to say," the old man said slowly as he scrunched his soda can in two, "that I wish you wouldn't call me Gumbo. I haven't used that name in years."

Connie leaned against the door jamb. "Since when?"

"Not for years."

"Pierre? Do you want me to call you that? Your first name?"

Border rose. "He uses his middle name."

"Crosby?" she said after a moment.

"Yes," said Border's father.

Paul shifted and his thigh rolled onto the TV's remote

control. The channel abruptly switched, and all eyes jerked to the set as a dark picture from the local access station filled the screen. Where there had been a war, now little girls danced in recital.

"Crosby," whispered Paul.

"Oh, honey," Connie said. "For almost forty years I've called you Gumbo."

"Jeff and Maud call him Crosby," Border said. "And how about that Scotch?"

"Not when they're talking to me," said Connie, ignoring the rest. "Forty years. Why you got that name when . . . when . . . I can't even remember."

"I'll fix the drinks," said Border. "How do I do it?"

Paul shifted again, thigh on remote, and the war resumed.

"Whatever," Border's father said. "I guess I don't care."

Connie leaned over and kissed his head. She straightened. "Can't believe how much gray hair you boys have." The gray-haired boy, not her own, stood and they hugged.

"Time will tell about this war, I guess," he said.

"Hope for the best."

"Crosby," Paul whispered again. "What a great name." He tapped rapidly on the keyboard.

Border went into the kitchen and helped Connie fix cocoa.

Protest —

The next day a demonstration began during fifth period, but Border didn't know anything was happening because at that moment he was in the nurse's office, sitting in his briefs and staring at a poster on infant nutrition while the nurse, Mrs. Neelon, swabbed ointment on his left thigh.

Fifteen minutes earlier, in the middle of science lab, Michaela Engle had spilled acid.

"Oops," she'd said as she stumbled and the clear liquid sloshed out of the vial onto Border's thigh, where it sizzled and smoked and burned holes through the denim.

He watched the burning, speechless, his eyes getting wider when the acid reached flesh.

"Geez and crackers!" he groaned at last.

"Sorry," said Michaela. "At least those are old jeans."

"True," Border said stiffly. "But it's a new leg."

"Maybe I should just go home," he said to the nurse.

"Can't do that," she answered cheerfully. "I had Joyce wash the acid off those pants and now they're in the dryer."

"You have a dryer in school?"

"You bet. A washer, too. We're always cleaning up kids. Vomit, mostly. This is the first time we've done acid." She straightened, turned away, froze. "Oh my goodness, look at that! What's going on? Joyce, come here!" Her aide ran from the outer office and the two women looked out the window while Border sat in his underwear.

"Whatever are they doing?" Joyce said.

"Border, come look."

"Uh, Mrs. Neelon . . ."

She gave him a paper sheet. Border wrapped it around his waist and joined them at the window.

Two stories down and across the street a group of students had gathered on the lawn of a house. A stream of kids flowed out of the high school, straight below the nurse's office. A few held hand-lettered signs, and Border saw three girls unroll a long banner: NO GUNS FOR OIL, it said, and was decorated with peace signs and flowers. He frowned. Bad artwork.

57

"Shameful," Joyce said, and the nurse agreed.

"Though," she responded, "they have the right to their opinion."

"Not in wartime," Joyce said crisply. "That's the same as treason. They should be suspended. Walking out and doing this!"

"Did you hear the president last night?"

"He was wonderful!"

They exited to the outer office and Border stood watching alone. Maybe thirty kids out in the cold. Shouting, chanting, smoking, kicking at chunks of snow. A car pulled up and parked. Men got out. Cops?

VETS FOR PEACE, their poster said; everybody cheered and high-fived, slapping palms reddened from cold.

One girl lounged against a tree trunk and flashed "V" with her fingers whenever a car drove by. The girl sort of looked like Dana, dressed like Dana. Border shivered. His thighs, bare under the sheet, popped goose pimples. He hoped his sister, wherever she was, was wearing more than paper.

The protest continued for the rest of fifth period and most of sixth. No cops came by, no school officials came out, and finally it broke up. A few kids lingered, smoking.

Border watched until Mrs. Neelon brought his dryer-hot jeans. He slipped them on and headed straight for the library. Study hall next period, why bother with geometry for fifteen minutes?

The library was deserted and he found a carrel next to the sci-fi and fantasy collection. The lurid cover of one book faced out and caught his eye: a voluptuous babe with her hand on the hero's hunky chest. *Canyons of Istabar*. Border pulled it off the shelf and began reading.

"You have some nerve, Baker, hanging around after that little show. You dumb-ass traitorous son of a bitch, son of a dope-brained coward."

Border's books had scattered in the snow. He spotted *Canyons* soaking up moisture as it lay in a slushy tire track. He'd finished seven chapters in the library, wanted to know the end. Probably unreadable now.

He blew out his nose and watched blood splatter on snow. Then he coughed, a quick succession of sharp gagging hacks, until the bloody phlegm was forced up into his mouth. He spat it out.

"A few punches," Bryan whined. He turned to his companions. "I didn't even hit him that hard." His friends murmured agreement. "I should have known he wouldn't fight back. Chicken."

Border pushed up and inched back until he could rest against his car. "You're too tough for me, Bryan."

A wad of spit landed on Border's shoe.

Border closed his eyes, tapped on his thighs. "Why are you doing this? I got your message yesterday. You don't like me. I understand."

"I wanted you to know what I think of your little demonstration today."

"Huh?" he honked. "I wasn't there."

Bryan frowned. "I heard you walked out during fifth period, the first one to leave. You weren't in geometry, I know that."

Border started to speak, then shut up. He owed the bastard nothing.

Bryan nodded. "Just what I thought."

"You know, Bryan, until about two minutes ago I didn't hate you, even after you jumped me yesterday." He shifted, stifled a moan. Man, his jaw hurt. "After all, your jokes in class aren't half-bad. Whoa, easy now, don't kick me. Are you going to kick me?"

Bryan squinted. "I should. I should kick you back to New Mexico."

Something dripped across Border's lips. He wiped it with the back of his hand, leaving a dark smear on light gray gloves. "Gosh, Bryan, I doubt if even a fine athlete like you could do that."

The kicks came hard, and Border crumpled over, thinking as his head hit ground, *I am so stupid*.

"Stop it," one of Bryan's friends whispered. There was murmuring, then footsteps in snow, and Border was alone.

He rose slowly and leaned against the car, sorry for himself. Dark sky, dirty snow, sharp wind, foul mood.

Get in the car, drive home. New Mexico. What was stopping him?

Border looked at his bloody glove. Life with mother, that's what. Life with someone who puts that life on stage. What would she do with this? Hold him and clean the blood?

"Nope," said Border aloud. "She'd put it in a show. She'd start writing. She'd —"

He wasn't alone. Another boy stood watching, ten feet away. Border raised his arms. "Go ahead, kick me."

"Is that what happened? You're a mess. Who did it?"

Border brushed snow off his jacket. "Pack of little girls, seven or eight of them. Vicious things. Beat me with their Barbie dolls."

"Think you need to see a doctor? The hospital —"

"No!" Right into his father's lair? No. "I'm okay. It's probably just a bloody nose."

"I live a block over from your house. I could use a ride home."

Border frowned. Did everyone know who he was?

"I work at the grocery store and I saw you shopping with Mrs. Sanborn. I've cut her lawn for years."

Border tossed his keys to the boy. "I've got blood caked on my eye and my head hurts. You drive."

A cautious driver; Border got impatient. Tapped on his thighs.

"What are you doing?"

"What?"

"With your fingers."

"Watch the road. Gosh, people drive slowly in this town."

"No place to go, why go fast?"

"What's your name?"

"Jacob McQuillan. Not Jake."

"Border Baker, but you know that. I play recorder. Sometimes I get songs in my head and the fingers move. Habit."

"My sister's birthday was yesterday. There's leftover cake. Want some?"

Border's stomach responded. "Cake would be good," he said.

Jacob parked in the driveway of a small house similar to Border's, but painted white. He gave Border the car keys, then leaned over and looked at the wound on Border's face. "What a mess."

"Are the cuts bad?"

"No cuts at all. I think you were right — the blood came from your nose." He shifted closer, looking.

"Whoa, Jacob. Another inch and I'll have to kiss you."

Pandemonium at the door. Seventy pounds of Labrador pounced. Border cringed, the dog leaped, ran in circles, barked, then sat on its haunches and howled: *Ah-rooo.*

"She's glad to see us," said Jacob.

"I guess," said Border.

Jacob held open the door. "Out, Pooch. Go do your thing."

They ate cake straight out of the pan, holding it between them, two forks digging in. Pooch returned, put her paws up on the door and licked the glass until Jacob let her in.

They ate and talked. Jacob was a junior. Had played hockey until knee surgery. Worked on the school paper. Parents were teachers. Five younger sisters.

"So I was ready to believe you," he said, "when you told me about the Barbie dolls."

Border talked less, holding back. Jacob knew most of the story anyway. After all, he'd cut grass for Connie.

He didn't know about Dana.

"We're not too worried," said Border. "It's sort of like her to do something like this."

"But what if she's been hurt?"

"Then we'll be sorry."

They finished the cake and Jacob set the pan down for Pooch. She licked furiously, pushing it around the floor, nose stuck in the corners, searching for crumbs.

Three sisters came home, two of them fighting. They carried the fight through the kitchen and into their bedroom. The oldest sister stopped, dumping books on the table.

"What happened to you?" she asked Border.

"Liz, meet Border. Border, meet Liz," said Jacob.

"He's in three of my classes. What happened?"

Border needed a moment. Three classes? He couldn't think of one.

"Geometry, Resources, History. What happened?"

"Some guys jumped me. Really only one guy, I guess, but the others were watching."

"What guy?" she asked over her shoulder, as she stood at the fridge and poured milk.

"He's not telling."

He told. "Bryan someone."

Liz and Jacob groaned. "Bryan Langtry, I bet," she said. "Figures. Stupid. Stupid guys. Hey, where's the cake?"

Pooch flicked a paw and the pan skidded across the floor. Liz scowled at her brother and picked up the pan. "This was my cake," she said.

"Sorry," said her brother.

"Happy birthday," said Border. "A day late."

"Guys," said Liz as she left the room, "are such jerks."

The fighting sisters returned to the kitchen. The short one looked at Border. "Gross," she said. The other one nodded.

"Time to go," said Border. Jacob and Pooch walked him out to the car. "Do you like hockey?" Jacob asked. "There's a home game Friday."

"I've never seen a hockey game."

"Lotta fun. Around here it's bigger than basketball. Whole town goes."

Bryan and his buddies? "I don't know."

"Think about it."

In the car, Border rolled down the window and leaned out. "Thanks for helping."

Jacob flipped his hand. "I needed the ride."

He went straight to the phone machine. Nerve center of the family. Light flashed. Word from Dana? No, just Dad. *Dinner with friends, then some tennis. Home by ten. Here's something to think about: Should we join the Y?*

Y not?

He called his mother's machine, spoke to it: Any news? I haven't heard anything.

Family life, the nineties.

He washed and changed clothes. Checked his wounds. Bruises on a thigh and hip. Face wasn't too bad, which was good: no cuts, no gashes, no questions. His dirty shirt was blood-stained and he threw it away, shoving it to the bottom of the trash. His hand came up smelling like old spinach. Washed again.

Supper alone, watching the war. Fiery skies, tense reporters, gas masks, sirens.

Border muted the sound and played his recorder. Rolling Stones, an oldie, "Sympathy for the Devil."

Telephone call for Gumbo. "He's playing tennis," said Border.

"The party's set for Saturday. Let him know."

Border promised, said good-bye.

Zzzip flash, zzzip flash, missiles over the Middle East. Pyroball, bigtime. Border played Mozart. Too pretty.

Telephone for Gumbo. "Did he hear about the party?"

"He will," Border promised.

Zzzip flash. Border touched his tender face. Telephone for Gumbo, did he hear about the beating? Telephone for Gumbo, did he hear about the kicking? Telephone for Gumbo, did he hear about the bleeding?

Brahms? No, still too pretty. Border whacked the recorder against his palm. Stupid instrument, really. Drums would be better. A big kettledrum, a bass drum. Nothing pretty, no melody, no song, no oldies. Just hit it and hit it and hit it.

Red, White, and Blue —

Flags everywhere. After just a few days of war, they had sprouted all over town. Front porches, car antennas, picture windows. On Sunday afternoon Border erected a pole for Connie and Paul outside their house. Fifteen feet of aluminum weighted down in a barrel of sand. An hour in the cold — red hands, numb toes, ringing ears — but finally the flag ran up the pole and flapped.

"Looks good," said Paul.

"Perfect, hon," said Connie.

"You could've worn gloves," said the old man, who hadn't helped at all but joined them in time for cocoa.

"Good advice, Gumbo," said Border. And out of the corner of his eye, he saw his father stiffen. Got the message: Not funny.

Didn't mean to be.

At school on Monday, more flags. Classrooms and hallways, tables in the lunchroom, backpacks and buttons. Someone had slapped a flag decal on Border's locker. He spent too much time trying to scrape it off and was late for math class. It didn't matter; no one noticed. When he walked in, people were crowded around a desk in the back.

Border slipped into his. Dug out his homework.

"Here, here," barked the teacher. "Order!" People sat down, still talking. "Quiet, or we have a quiz!" That worked.

The teacher clasped his hands. "So that we might all fully appreciate the patriotic effort of your classmate, why don't we ask Chandra to model her outfit?"

Border twisted in his seat — hard to do, he filled it up — as a girl in the back rose and walked down the aisle, displaying a short skirt and top she'd made out of a flag. The class cheered and whooped, clapped and snapped a rhythm for her walk. Border frowned, puzzled. Thought about the old man's stories from his days in high school when people were going nuts over the Vietnam War. Back then it was the protesters who wore the flag. And caught hell for it.

But now, 1991, some girl was sashaying through rows of desks wearing a flag over a black leotard. The class went wild. The teacher beamed. Border checked his homework.

Mrs. Zipoti —

"Hummus!"

Everyone came to attention. But then, as Border had learned his first day in school, everyone was always at attention in Mrs. Zipoti's class, Resources for Living. One slip, one slight drift toward daydream, and those eyes would zero in and that broad rock of a bosom would hover, extinguishing light and, very possibly, life.

"Does anyone know what hummus is?"

Gulag Zipoti, he'd learned to call the class the first day. And in any other class but the Gulag, Border suspected the usual jokes would have been whispered: Hummus a tune; Hummus is that doggie in the window?

Not a word. She licked her lips in satisfaction, having once again proven that students were dumb, dumber, dumbest.

"Hummus is a staple food of the Mideast. Today we will make hummus."

They made hummus. There were several Middle Eastern restaurants in Albuquerque, and Border had eaten hummus often, but he could tell the other kids hadn't. As everyone's bowls of gloppy beige paste developed, the groans and gagging started. Mrs. Zipoti beamed satisfaction from behind her counter.

"Through food," she intoned, "we can gain understanding, appreciation, and empathy for other cultures." Her chest heaved. "Even as we destroy them."

A whisper from the back: "People who have to eat this crap should beg to be bombed."

Mrs. Zipoti found the voice. She glided from her counter to where a girl slouched in a seat. Mrs. Z didn't say a word, just glared, breathed deeply, returned to her mount.

Border and the others could read her mind.

Big fat *F*.

Escape —

The next day Border ditched school. Between classes he caught Bryan eyeing him a few times, not friendly, and decided, Why wait for trouble?

It felt so good sitting in the car, out of the school, free to go. He drove away fast, headed nowhere.

He cruised Main. Still only morning, and there was no one to see but slow-moving senior citizens crossing the street at a crawl. Border stopped for one who paused in the middle of the street to search his pockets.

Honk, maybe, just to move him along? Better not — might

scare 'im to death. Border tapped on the steering wheel, looked around. On the courthouse grounds two men were tying a banner to trees. FUTURE SITE OF . . . The plastic flapped.

The car behind Border's honked. The old man quit his pocket search, looked up and scowled at Border, then raised a mittened fist before plodding on.

He drove the Volvo around the courthouse, parked, and got out to read the sign.

FUTURE SITE OF WALTHAM COUNTY WAR MEMORIAL. GROUNDBREAKING: MEMORIAL DAY, 1991. The banner included a drawing of the future monument — a plain stone wall, with room for names. Someone joined Border. "Sort of copying the Vietnam Memorial," Border said aloud, not looking at his companion.

"They could do worse than that."

"True." He turned to look and was eye to eye with a stern man in a uniform. A sheriff's deputy, according to the badge.

"Shouldn't you be in school, son?"

Yes, he should. "Going that way, after . . ." After what? A nap? A few hours of TV? ". . . the dentist."

The deputy smiled. "Wouldn't want to be in your shoes."

"No sir. Two fillings." Border nodded and walked to his car, sucking back a smile. Sometimes the lies came so easy.

Next morning, he slept until ten and woke up thinking, *I should be in school.* Fell back asleep.

Habit. Back home it was easy to ditch, they never checked. Two thousand kids in a school, who noticed?

This time, his father.

They called me at work, Border. Three surgeries scheduled, the place is wild, and I have to deal with a school secretary.

Nice lady.

I called three times this morning. Where were you? What did you do all day?

Slept.

I'm busting my butt earning a living for us and you're home sleeping.

Teenagers need sleep. Lots of it.

Give me your car keys.

What?

Punishment, Border. Consequences. You do not skip school.

Ground me or something, but let me drive.

Keys, please.

How do I get to school? Do you want me to stay home and sleep?

It's yellow. It stops at the corner. It's called a bus.

No!

Yes! Keys?

It's crowded, Dad. It's got *junior high* kids on it.

I don't care.

That's obvious. For how long?

Two weeks. You're not grounded, but you're not driving.

Two weeks without a car? You're kidding!

Dead serious.

No way. I won't.

You will. Know why? Because I can make things even worse. This house isn't a democracy. I'm the father, you're the kid, and I'm in charge. Keys, please.

After that, nothing to do but stay away from each other. Nothing to do but go to bed. While he brushed his teeth, Border remembered the phone machine. The old man said he'd phoned in the morning, but there had been a call in the afternoon. He'd heard the ringing from his room and hadn't bothered to play any messages later, certain they were all from his dad.

Sure enough — one from the school secretary, then three calls from his father.

Beep number five and his head jerked with the hello.

Hello, gorgeous guys. I bet you don't have any idea where I am. I'm not so sure I do, exactly speaking, but I do know I'm having an adventure. Here's what happened: I got off the plane in Atlanta, right? And there was this sign that said "Welcome to Atlanta. Visit the World of Coca-Cola." Coke is my poison, you know that, so I figured, what the heck, New Mexico can wait. I got a cab and took the tour and saw how they made the stuff. Only it wasn't the real factory, just a fake one for the tour, but it was still pretty neat. And there were these women on the tour — you know the type, Old Town tourists with white hair, jogging suits, sneakers — and they said the World of Coke was almost as good as the Hershey chocolate plant in — where else? — Hershey, Pennsylvania. So I figured I oughta see that. My grandparents — oh boy, Border, wait till you hear about them — gave me all this money, so don't worry about me, Dad. Anyway, wait, I need to stuff a few quarters . . .

Okay. I'm in Pennsylvania, at least for the next thirty minutes, then the bus leaves. Bus tickets are so much cheaper than airfare. Think I can get a refund on the part of the ticket I didn't use? By the way, those women were wrong. The Hershey tour was a dud. Coke was much better. So, how's Minnesota? How's the job, Dad? Everything okay? Were you guys worried about me? Sorry about that. Would you mind calling Mom? Thanks. See ya.

Dana.

Out and In —

Border and his father argued about who would make the call to New Mexico.

"She's your sister, it's your mother, you call."

"I'm going to bed. After all, you're in charge."

Border took an atlas to his room. Dana had piled up credits in high school and graduated a semester early. "I want to get out and get going," she'd told Border. He found Atlanta and then Hershey on the map. He closed his eyes and circled his finger over North America. "She could be going here." Tap. Tennessee. "Or here." Tap. Maine. "Here." Tap. Oops, the Arctic Circle. Maybe not.

He thought about his father's grim smile when he'd pocketed the Volvo keys. So pleased with himself, so glad he'd devised a suitable punishment. In charge. Border tapped the map on Minnesota. "Me," he said. "Here."

Dana was out, Dana was going.

Border was in, Border was stuck.

Hey, Jacob, okay if I sit here?

Sure. You guys met Border? Chuck chuck chuck chuck chuck. Move over for him. You move over. What is this stuff, beef barf? Anyone done with those math problems? Lookit Jenny K.; lookit that body; please, just once in my life. You make your own lunch? Don't New Mexicans have accents? Maybe it's pork puke. How come you walked to school? Screw the problems; I'll be in summer school anyway. Who's going to the game? Is New Mexico where the Grand Canyon is? Presser is the worst math teacher. Do you speak Spanish? I ditched once, ran into my grandmother at the video store. Who can drive to the game? Not Chuck. His name is Border, bugbrain. There's the bell. Border Bugbrain? I thought it was Baker.

Friday Night —

It was cold in the hockey arena. Border zipped his jacket, bummed some gloves, then borrowed a scarf, and still he was cold. He stamped his feet until they hurt, hunched his shoulders, hugged himself. Around him, a thousand fans screamed and cheered, shooting up and down in the seats. Border shivered.

Jacob took pity and suggested they leave. "I should have warned you that it's cold in here. Long underwear is usually a good idea."

"We can stay. I'm okay."

"You're freezing. Besides, it's not worth it. Red Cedar will never make up four goals. We've lost this one."

Jacob had consumed three sodas and needed the bathroom. Border waited for him in the arena lobby, amusing himself by flipping a quarter. Heads, tails, heads, tails, tails, tails. The quarter slipped off his thumb, hit concrete, and spun. He picked it up, straightened, and spotted Bryan and two companions watching him.

Border looked at the bathroom door. Where was Jacob? Zip, pee, zip — how long could it take? He eyed the three. He was bigger than any of them. Six-one, one-eighty. Go ahead, guys; this time he wasn't rolling over.

"You stupid jerks, are you actually going to fight again?"

Liz leaned against the doorway to the girl's john. Border smiled and relaxed. Saved. By a girl.

"Clarissa was looking for you, Bryan."

"Yeah?"

"Yeah. She said you said you'd be here."

"I am."

"She's sitting by Jenny and the others. Michael's there, too."

"Michael?" Bryan stiffened. "Why's he sitting by her?"

Liz shrugged.

Bryan mumbled something and led his friends away.

"Poor Michael," said Border.

"Where's Jacob? I saw the two of you leaving. I need a ride."

"Bathroom. He's — oh, there. That took long enough."

"Don't get so personal," said Jacob.

"Can I have a ride home?" Liz asked.

"I thought you were with Heidi and Kris tonight."

"I was, but ten minutes into the first period Heidi got back together with Jeremy, and then Kris heard about this party that Brett might go to. I don't want to party, so now I need a ride."

"Geez," said Border. "Michael and Clarissa and Bryan, and Heidi and Jeremy, and . . . and . . ."

"Prince Charles and Di," helped Jacob.

"Is stuff like that important around here?"

"Stuff?" Liz asked.

"Dating, going together."

"Only one thing's bigger," said Jacob.

The crowd roared, the building shook, probably a Red Cedar goal.

"Hockey?"

Jacob tossed and caught his car keys. "Food. Let's get some."

Remembering —

Liz and Jacob couldn't agree on a restaurant. Border listened to the argument for a while as they drove around town, then said, "I'm pretty much broke. Let's just go to my house. Dad got groceries last night."

Jacob wasn't shy and immediately hunted in the fridge and cupboards for something to eat. Liz looked elsewhere. Dropping her coat on a chair, slipping out of her shoes, she exclaimed, "It's so weird! This house is exactly like ours, only it's not." She wandered out of view, looking.

Border sat idly while the brother and sister busied themselves in his house.

Jacob made a huge, everything-in-it omelet.

"Gosh, Jacob," his sister said when he called her back to the kitchen. "Make yourself at home, why don't you?"

"Don't you want any?"

She lifted plates from a shelf. "I hope you used garlic."

They kept it up while eating. Border liked the banter; it reminded him of being with Dana.

"Found your sister yet?" Jacob asked.

Border's jaw dropped and egg spilled.

"That's not attractive," Liz said. "Close your mouth."

"Sorry. It's just, well, I was thinking of her at that exact moment," said Border. "The question surprised me."

"I think you should call the police," said Jacob.

"We've prayed for her," said Liz. Jacob made a soft unhappy noise.

"You what?"

"During our family prayers, we said one for her."

"Now he's going to think we're really weird, Liz."

"What are your family prayers?"

"What do you think? Every day before supper, we get together and say a few prayers. Can you handle it?"

Border speared a mushroom with his fork. "Sure. You'll probably think I'm weird: I've never been to church. Not once."

Liz shrugged. "Families are different."

Jacob dropped his fork and lifted his glass of orange juice. "I'll drink to that."

"Well, maybe your prayers worked," Border said after they toasted, "because my sister has turned up. No one's actually seen her, but she left a message on the phone machine the other day. It's like we thought — she had to transfer planes in Atlanta and she decided she wasn't going home. I don't know where she is right now, but I'm pretty sure she's okay."

"Do you miss her?" Liz asked.

"Impossible," said her brother.

"Sort of," said Border. "We didn't live together, not since my parents broke up."

"Do you miss New Mexico?" asked Liz.

"Yes."

"I've only ever lived in Red Cedar," said Liz, "and we've hardly ever traveled. What's New Mexico like?"

Border took his time thinking about it all. What do you tell two small-town kids who pray every day with their family? Should he tell them about his friends and the hours they'd spend together drifting through the university campus or the nearby stores where they'd check out the comics, used books, vintage clothing? Or tell them how he liked to watch Alonzo at work in his body-piercing salon? Tell them about the coffee shops where he'd set out his hat and play until he'd earned enough money to feed all his friends? And pyroball? Border looked at their smooth, unblemished hands, used for praying, never singed.

They wouldn't get it.

"New Mexico is pretty," he said. "I miss the mountains."

"We have a mountain in Red Cedar," said Liz.

"What?" said Jacob.

"Where?" asked Border.

"There's a nature preserve," said Liz. "And there's this mountain there."

"She's joking," said Jacob. "It's just a giant boulder."

"I've climbed it," she said.

"You haven't," said her brother.

"Have too."

"When?"

"Hundreds of times."

"Hundreds?"

"Often enough. Have you? Betcha can't."

"Course I can."

"Try it."

"I don't do things just because there's a dare."

"Try it. Tonight."

Jacob frowned. "Rock climbing at night? That's stupid."

"I'm up for it," said Border.

Liz moaned. "That was awful."

"What?"

"Your joke. It was a terrible pun."

"Huh?"

"You are as dense as my brother. *Up* for it? Rock climbing?"

"You can't be serious, Border," said Jacob. "An hour ago you were freezing to death."

Border stacked plates. "I'm warmed up now. And besides," he said, "I'll put on long underwear."

Dogs in Baghdad —

"Porter's Park Preserve," said Liz, as they drove along a dark road into a deserted parking lot, "was made possible by Porter's Pork."

"That's a good one," said Border. "Say it three times real fast: Porter's Pork preserves Porter's Park Preserve."

They tried, they failed. They were laughing when Jacob parked the car.

"I'm not sure we're supposed to be here after hours," said Liz. "Maybe this wasn't a good idea."

"Maybe it wasn't *whose* good idea?" asked her brother.

"My idea," said Border. "Let's do it."

"A flashlight might be nice," said Jacob. And he leaned across Border's lap and opened the glove compartment. "Here we go and . . . Voilà! It even works. Hooray for Mom and Dad; they're always prepared."

"Not always," said Liz as she opened the rear door. "That's how they ended up with six kids."

Jacob directed the flashlight beam along a trail of packed snow. Border followed the others, vowing, as he slipped and snow spilled into his shoes, to buy boots the next day.

The boulder loomed over the path, a massive shadow.

"What do you think, twenty feet to the top?" asked Border.

"If that."

"There's a plaque on it that tells . . ." said Liz, and she took the light from her brother. "Here."

Border leaned to read.

Glacial Erratic

The boulder before you is probably one of the oldest objects you'll ever touch. Geologists have dated rocks of this type at 3.6 billion years. At that time pressures deep within the earth changed the boulder from granite into gneiss. This process occurred in an area that is now the Minnesota River Valley, ninety miles northwest of this spot. Less than half a million years ago, a lobe of an ancient glacier plucked this boulder from the surrounding bedrock, then transported and deposited it at a site just north of the preserve. It was uncovered during the construction of the interstate highway. This glacial erratic measures 20 × 17 × 11 feet and weighs about 125 tons.

"Hey," said Border, "that's me. It's talking about me."

Jacob laughed, but Liz said, "I don't get it. Because you're big?"

"Now who's dense?" said her brother. He pointed to the plaque. "Like the rock, Border was picked up and dumped in Red Cedar. He doesn't belong here."

"Do you really feel that way?" asked Liz.

"I feel," said Border, looking up and running his hands along the rock, "that maybe I can do this." He started climbing.

He'd climbed rocks often enough in the hills outside Albuquerque, though never at night. Still, climbing was mostly touch and balance and strength. He could hear Jacob behind him, breathing hard and grumbling.

Border reached the top, breathless, hands cold and scraped.

"Hello," said Liz cheerfully. "That took a while."

Her brother swung a leg over the top, pulled himself up.

"How did you get up here ahead of us?" said Border.

"There's an easy way up the back. It's practically a path. If you guys had waited, I would have told you. But no, you moron males had to charge ahead."

Jacob rubbed his hands and swore at Liz. Border grinned. "I wish my sister were here. I bet you two would be friends."

"Do you like your sister?" Liz asked.

"More or less. Depends on her hair color." He looked around. Not much to see but a starry sky and dark patches where the trees were.

"What do we do now?" said Jacob.

"Enjoy it," said Liz.

"How do we get down?" he wondered.

"Relax, would you?"

"Slide on our butts, probably," said Border. "Liz can lead the way."

Liz lifted her arm and pointed. "If I led you that way, we'd come to a creek." She shifted slightly. "That way to New Mexico and," she moved again, "that way to Kuwait."

"Weird, isn't it?" said Border. "To think that while we're sitting here with nothing to do but get cold, there's a war going on."

"No one's looking at stars in Iraq," said Liz.

"Probably it's already day there," said Jacob.

"Then they're looking at bomb damage," said Border.

"There's no way," Jacob said, "that you would not go crazy. I mean, if where you lived was being bombed. Killed or crazy — some options."

"The noise must be incredible," said Border. "The sound of the missiles coming down, then exploding. One after another — you'd hear them and wait for one, maybe the next one, to hit you."

"Like I said, you'd go crazy."

"Pooch certainly would," said Liz. "She can't handle a thunderstorm. First crack and she's under the table whining."

"*I* don't want to whine," said Jacob, "but is anyone else cold?"

"Sure," said Liz. "It's winter."

"I'm sort of cold," said Border. "I suppose it would be smart to go."

No one moved. They sat, looking and listening, seeing only stars and hearing nothing more than a soft wind through bare tree branches.

"If you were in a war," Border asked, "would you bother to save your pet? Do people leave pets behind to go to a bomb shelter?"

"Don't know," said Jacob.

"Do other cultures even have pets? I mean kids in other places, do they have dogs or cats? Are there Labradors in Iraq?"

"I've never thought about it," said Liz.

"And if there are pets and they get killed during the bombing, do they get buried?" Jacob asked. "Or can't people take the time to do that?"

"Probably not," said Border.

Jacob nodded. "Maybe they just get the bulldozers and —"

Liz pounded on her brother's arm. "Stop that. What an awful thought."

They quieted. Border was cold, but he didn't want to leave, didn't want to move. Just sat there with the others, watching the clear, peaceful sky. Thinking about war, thinking about dogs in Baghdad.

—∾—

Snow, snow, and more snow. On Monday Border walked out of the school and got it slapped in his face. Turned to the person next to him, no one he knew, and snarled, "I hate Minnesota." She hustled away.

The buses were lined up, stinky exhaust choking everyone. Since losing his keys, Border had walked to school, rising early, getting home late. Two cold miles, but he had survived.

"It's gonna be a blizzard," he heard through the noise, and looked down to see Liz.

"No school tomorrow?"

"We can hope."

He followed her onto a bus. It was packed, three to a seat. Jacob waved from the back. Border nodded, then he sat behind Liz, wedging in beside two skinny kids, junior high types.

The kids started tussling. Border got bumped.

Boys behind him kicked the seat.

Something flew through the air. The driver shouted and closed the door. The bus lurched and pulled away, and a girl in the aisle fell into Border's lap.

"Gawd!" she said and hurried away.

"Get a feel?" one of his seatmates asked.

Border stared at Liz's hair. There was a piece of string just above her collar. He poised his fingers to pick it off and just then the boys slugged each other, bumping him. His hand grazed her neck.

She turned around. "*What* are you doing?"

"There was some string on your hair."

"Don't bother, Border."

The boys giggled. Border cooled them off with a stare. "I can hurt you now," he said, "or I can hurt you later. Or you can be quiet."

They shut up and sat still the rest of the ride.

All He Wanted —

Border got off with Liz and Jacob.

"Come over?" said Jacob. "There's another cake."

Border's stomach growled, and he nodded.

Pooch met them at the door, paws and tongue on the glass, tail whacking the floor. *Woof woof, woof woof, ah-rooo!* She went outside when the door opened and ran circles in the snow.

Liz joined them to eat cake, three forks attacking the pan.

"Border made a pass at me on the bus," she said to her brother.

"I'm sure you liked it," he replied.

Border reached, lifted string off her hair. "*This* was all I wanted," and he dropped it on the table.

Wind pelted snow against the windows. Border plunged his fork into the cake. It was nice and warm in this kitchen.

Oh, No —

At home he was alone. He made a sandwich for supper, turned on the TV. The local weather man predicted snow. Border looked out to where it was piling up.

"And now our special report," the anchor said, stumbling

over those simple words. "We have four guests in the studio tonight who will share their stories of how war changes lives."

Border looked up from making a second sandwich and saw his father on the screen.

Discipline, II —

You could have told me about this; you could have asked me.

They called me at work. I didn't have time.

You know what trouble I'll get at school?

How bad can it be?

I have been kicked, Dad. I have been jumped and punched and kicked.

What? Why didn't you tell me?

You weren't around. You didn't notice.

Is that why you're mad? Is that the real reason?

You don't notice your kid's been slugged, but, boy, your tennis game's getting better.

You're feeling pretty darn sorry for yourself.

Why shouldn't I?

Why should you? What is so awful about your life?

It's in the wrong place.

Don't walk away from me. Don't you dare slam your door. You slam that door and —

Bang!

— you're grounded!

—∽—

In Red Cedar, Minnesota, what's there to miss when you're grounded? A hockey game? Back home there was stuff to miss. The stores, parties, driving up into the foothills, hiking, the tourist crowds in Old Town tossing money into his hat, late nights with friends.

He'd been grounded once before, for driving when he was fifteen, no license. His parents had a long phone consultation about appropriate and effective punishment. He'd listened to his father's end of it for a while, then left, staying out with friends and on the street for three days and two nights, then coming home to find out he was grounded.

Wow, discipline! Okay, Dad.

He had been tired, anyway, needed to catch up on his sleep and practice his music. That was the first time.

This time, could he tell the difference? Border lay on his bed in the house in Red Cedar and thought not.

After an hour in his room, Border went back to the kitchen. His father was reading the paper. Border poured milk, drank it in loud slurps. He burped.

Jacob called and said school had been canceled for the next day because of the snow. Did he want to go to the preserve and try cross-country skiing?

"Can't go," Border said, making sure his father heard. "I'm grounded."

Connie called. Could he help with the shoveling?

"Can't help you, Connie," Border said. "I'm grounded."

His father grabbed the phone from him and said, "He'll do anything you need, anytime."

"So I'm not grounded from everything?" Border asked.

"Except for school and helping. You can still do that."

Later, he listened from his bedroom while his father talked on the phone to his friend.

"Cripes, Jeff, I haul him off to a new town and he gets beat up and all I'm smart enough to do is scream my head off. What a screwup. I am so good at that, you know? I don't care what Diana's life is like these days, maybe it would be better for him to be with her . . . Don't try to tell me that, I know when I'm failing . . ."

Border buried his head under his pillows. He'd heard enough.

Helping —

"Are you still grounded? Can you do something tonight?" Liz wrapped her arms around her backpack. "It's been a week."

Border nodded. "He didn't say for how long, so I guess I'm still in trouble. Or maybe he just forgot. That's possible. Dad's not very experienced at being tough, and he's probably trying to forget about it."

"What did you do that was so bad?" she asked.

"I slammed a door."

Jacob gasped and Liz covered her mouth. "Not the dreaded door slam!" said Jacob.

Border nodded. "Worst of all sins." The bus engine churned and they bounced in their seats. "What did you have in mind about tonight?"

Liz glanced at her brother. "Something at our church."

"No thanks."

"Don't panic. It's not religious," she said. But people are getting together at the church to pack up stuff to send to the soldiers in the Gulf. Our mom's kind of behind it. They've got all these donations from stores, and she's worried there won't be enough people to get the stuff boxed up."

"There'll be food," said Jacob. "Some of the ladies are really good cooks."

"But if you're grounded, never mind," said Liz.

"What kind of food?"

"The best," said Jacob. "There's one woman who makes these great tortes."

"It's not just eating, right? There's work to do? You might say I'd be *helping?*"

Liz nodded. "Definitely."

Border smiled. "Then I can go."

Church Basement —

"Nothing to eat until you've worked for an hour."

Jacob turned to Border. "This is my mother."

The woman tucked strands of hair back under a bandanna. "Nice to meet you at last, Border. Glad you came. Your father didn't mind?"

"He wouldn't." Not exactly, that is. If he knew, which he didn't. Border hadn't told him, hadn't even seen him.

"You mean he doesn't know you're here?"

"He was doing something tonight, so I couldn't ask."

Mrs. McQuillan frowned. Border smiled. "How can we help?"

Heavy labor, they were good for that. Border and Jacob

set up tables and chairs, then unloaded donated goods from a van. They carried a full coffee urn out of the kitchen. It leaked on Border's jeans.

A gray-haired woman, tall as Border and many pounds heavier, swooped up to the refreshment table. "Just what I need! Here boys, do something with this while I get myself a cuppa Joe." She handed Jacob a cloth-covered pan. He lifted the cloth and smiled. Chocolate torte.

By the time they took a break, the room had filled with people. Border and Jacob carried their plates and glasses and sat where they could give advice to Liz, who was working with five women assembling mailing boxes.

"Get to work," she said. "We have a thousand of these to tape together."

"We've been busy," said Border.

"Men's work," said Jacob.

"Nothing that needs brains!" quipped one of the women, and her companions laughed.

"Gotcha," said Liz.

"Saw your dad on the news last week," another woman said to Border. He frowned. How did she know him? Had they been introduced?

"I'm Dot Tully. His pop's that Vietnam draft dodger," she said to the others. One or two nodded.

"Fred and Maureen's boy?" a woman next to Border asked. "He's back in town?"

"Living right in their own same house," Dot Tully said. "Let me tell you — what's your name, exactly? Boomer, something like that?"

Jacob and Liz chuckled.

"It's Border."

"Well, Border, listening to your pop on that news show was a revelation. It was the first time I thought that what he did made sense. Not that I think going to Canada was right, but I understand it now. Understand *him* is maybe what I mean."

"Vietnam," said the woman next to Border, "was a mistake."

"Be careful what you say and how loud you say it," another woman answered. "Look around. Why, I bet almost every man in this room is a veteran of World War Two." Heads turned, eyes scanned.

"That was different. That was Hitler."

"Time sure changes how you look at things," a woman said.

"True," said Dot. "Still, I was a bit surprised," she said to Border, "to see you here helping."

"He's *not* helping," said Liz, and she took his plate and exchanged it for some box flats and tape. "Be useful, Boomer."

"Why were you surprised?" Border asked Dot Tully. Be pleasant, he ordered himself.

"Well, you being the son of your father. What would you expect?"

Expectations —

Expectations. He lived with them; everyone did. He knew that. Border never felt sorry for himself or anything. Not really. But it was tiresome.

Guy your size, what sports do you play?

A musician? Got a band, right? Smash guitars, that sort of thing?

You *don't* skateboard?

Dana's brother? You smart?

Diana's son? You write?

Gumbo's boy? Run, chicken, run!

Closing Up –

"Four hundred packages!" Mrs. McQuillan said. "That's twice as many as we'd hoped to get done tonight. We'll finish the others next week, then start our letter-writing project."

"Why wait until next week?" Dot Tully asked. "Let's meet again on Thursday — let's come twice a week. Everybody, whatcha think?"

A quick vote was taken, and it was agreed to meet Mondays and Thursdays; then it was also decided with a show of hands to have a few people plan future projects.

"We need a name," the chocolate torte woman said. "We need a checking account, too, for contributions so people don't end up paying out of their own pockets."

Names were suggested, but nothing appealed to everyone. Then, "I've got it," said the torte woman. "Local Involvement in our Country's Military."

People grumbled.

"Don't you get it? We'd be L-I-C-M: Lick 'em!"

Oh . . . Yeah! The name was approved.

Border frowned. Lick 'em. Sounded a little obscene.

He and Jacob loaded the finished care packages into a

van and stowed supplies in a closet. Tables put away, dishes cleared and washed. Still, people didn't rush home. Someone turned on a TV and people pulled up chairs around it. Talking, mostly, with minimal attention to the screen. Border wished he had his recorder and his hat. He was so broke. Would they think it weird? His fingers tapped.

"Music again?" said Jacob, sidling up.

Border started to explain what he'd been thinking about — playing for money. Would they cough anything up, he wanted to know.

"Isn't that sort of like begging?" Jacob asked.

Border shrugged. "I guess. I didn't really mean it."

A soap commercial gave way to news from the Gulf, and people stopped talking. The big, bald general appeared. He spoke precisely and calmly about the war.

Border was as enchanted as the others. The general was a mesmer. Cool, competent, manly. The perfect father.

Discipline, Interrupted —

I don't like being disobeyed.

I didn't.

What are you saying? I come home at ten and you're not here. You've been grounded, kid, what do you think that means?

You set the rules; I was following them.

Where the hell were you?

Do you have to yell? Schwarzkopf doesn't yell, Dad, and he's running a war.

Don't get smart, Border. Where were you?

I was helping. When you grounded me, there were two exceptions: school and helping. I was helping.

You weren't at Connie and Paul's. I called and got them all worried.

I was at church.

What?

Making care packages for the soldiers. Helping. Got it? Helping the war effort, Dad. Proud of me? Everyone there knew you, Dad. The Vietnam draft dodger.

What's going on, Border? Is this some little revenge game?

You tell me.

I should . . . I oughta . . .

Hit me? Course not. Send me to Santa Fe?

I've thought about it.

Would you be happier then? Dump me on her? Just get rid —

"Would you two shut up! I was sleeping."

Then There Were Three —

"Dana!"

Border stood still, while the old man lurched forward and hugged her. "You could have let us know you were coming," he said, still holding her.

She wiggled loose and turned to her brother. "I can't believe your hair. It's gone!"

"Lost it in Missouri."

"Gawd, Border, it's so sexy."

"Great. Just what I want to hear from my sister."

"Where have you been?" his father asked.

"Didn't you get the message I left?"

"We did," said Border, "but that was over a week ago."

"Battle Creek, Michigan. I love Corn Flakes, right? So after I toured Coke and Hershey, I thought it'd be cool to see how they make my favorite breakfast food. It was pretty amazing; they give away these toys on the tour, like the kind they put in cereal boxes."

"Have you called your mother?"

"Should I? I suppose. I've been on the bus for days. Weeks, really. I took some side trips. I got held up in some small town in Michigan. This punk took fifty bucks off me. I couldn't believe it; he was a pip-squeak, no more than five-five or something. I mean I had at least six inches on him, and he just sneaks up outside the bus station and twists my arm and feels me up until he finds money. That's when I knew I was tired and wanted to get off the road. No way, with enough sleep, that I'd let some punk roll me."

"How did you get in the house?" asked Border.

"The lock is feeble, guys. I did it with my driver's license. Just slipped it in the door frame and, zip, I was in."

"How long are you staying?" he asked.

"I'm not *staying* here." Dana opened the fridge. "I'm living here."

Border didn't need to look at his father to know he had paled.

"Okay," said his father. "Whatever. That's okay."

Border rolled his eyes. What a general. "You can't have my room, Dana."

"Don't want it. I'm sleeping down in the basement. The sofa folds out and it's really nice, and I was sleeping perfectly until I heard the shouting."

"Call your mother."

"Couldn't you? Tell her I'm sleeping or something."

"She'll want to talk, Sis."

"Duh."

The phone rang. Border shook his head. His mother the mind reader, probably.

The old man picked it up. "Thanks for worrying, Connie. He's home. I'll tell you tomorrow. Here's another good one — Dana has showed up. Yes, here. Okay, good night."

Border slumped. "Dad."

"What?"

"It's too late for company."

"I didn't invite her over."

"Since when is it necessary to invite her?"

"What are you guys talking about?" Dana asked.

Border walked to the living room and looked out the window just as the garage across the street opened. Taillights flashed and the Cadillac backed down the driveway. Within a minute, Connie was at the door.

"Hello-ho, kids. I knew I just couldn't go to sleep tonight. First I was thinking about you, Border, and how your dad oughta wallop you good. And then I hear about Dana. Oh, hon, we've been worried about you. I'm Connie. Umm, that salad looks good."

"Have some," said Border's dad, glumly.

"Can't. Paul told me to stay just a minute. Actually he said I shouldn't come at all, but, well, here I am. Oh, Dana, you're gorgeous, Border's twin almost. But, sweetheart, green hair!"

Border smiled, watching his sister stiffen and pull up to her full seventy-two inches, head proudly lifted on the long, pale neck.

94

"What about it?" Dana said, making a point of looking down at Connie's copper top.

Connie's mouth flapped twice. Border sucked air, amazed: Connie was speechless.

Not forever, of course. "It's just . . . I thought . . . Oh, hon, why . . ." She smiled. "Why, with your complexion, I'd go with blue."

Confidante —

Knock, Knock.

"Are you decent?" Dana whispered outside Border's bedroom door.

"Yes, and I'm awake, if that matters."

She entered, switched on the light, sat on his bed.

"Come right in," he said.

She pointed to a half-empty bottle of sparkling water on the floor. "How old is that?"

"More than a day, less than a week."

"Good enough." She picked it up, twisted off the cap, and drank.

"Connie is really something," she said when she'd swallowed.

"That's an understatement. Wait till you get to know her; words will fail you. Did you call Mom?"

"All done. Got her machine, thankfully."

"She's been worried. Now she'll just be mad."

"I don't care. I had a good time on my trip. Now I'm here, and I'm staying."

"Dad is stunned."

"He'll get over it. How's he doing with the new life?"

95

"Fine. Finding lots of old friends."

"And you?"

Border shrugged. "Good days, bad days."

"What's a bad day?"

"Happens when I stop and think about how small this town is. I warn you — every move you make, people are watching."

Dana smiled. "I like being watched."

"You'll love it here, then."

She yawned. "I don't care if I love it or not. I just don't want to go back to Santa Fe. Don't want to go back to her."

"How bad can it be?"

"I don't see *you* rushing off to live with our mother."

"I wasn't allowed to, remember? They divvied us up."

Dana nodded. "Boys and girls, that was the split."

Border smiled. "I think they argued more about dividing the CD collection."

"True enough."

"So what's the problem with Mom?"

"I'll give you a clue: She's preparing a new show."

He made a face. "That gets intense."

"And you know what she's calling this one? *The Family Plot.*"

"Are we in it?"

"You need to ask?" She set down the water bottle. "I had to get out of there. When she's rehearsing, it's like the whole world revolves around what she's thinking, what she believes, what she wants to say."

"I think it's always worse after the show opens. Remember the time that arts reporter tracked us down in school?"

Dana nodded. "Right after she did the nude thing for the first time."

"Wanting our opinions on the obscenity charges. What a dork."

Dana sighed. "I suppose I should give her credit for being brave."

"She's also a good poet," said Border. "Give her credit for that, too."

"Oh sure, her writing is amazing. Her performance . . ." They both laughed.

"I guess I can understand why you'd be going crazy living with her — two loud, tall poets in one small apartment."

"She doesn't think I'm much of a poet."

"Don't be silly. Your stuff is good. Maybe a little long . . ." She punched his foot. "When I show her some of my writing, Border, it's like, 'Oh, sweetheart, that's lovely!' I hate to be patronized."

"She's not patronizing you; she's mothering you."

"I know what she's doing." Dana crossed her legs. "It wasn't just her work that was hard to handle. Lee has been around a lot, and they argue so much. I was tired of having their fights in my face. I had to get out." She grinned, rose, made a fist, and rubbed the shaved back of his head. "And I wanted to see you, widdle brudda."

"Go to bed."

"I will, but first get your recorder and play me a lullaby. My head is rattling with the noise of bus engines. I want music."

"I'm out of practice. I haven't been playing much."

She stood up, stretched. "Why not? You used to play for hours."

97

"I don't know. Maybe because it doesn't fit here. Maybe because it's something I used to do back home. People here think I'm weird enough." He crossed his arms behind his head. "I'll play when I need the money."

"Or when you need the music."

"That's deep. Goodnight, Dana. I have to go to school tomorrow."

"Sweet dreams." She left, closing the door behind her.

Border punched his pillows, making a nest for his head. He dropped back down, smiling. Good to have someone to talk to.

Fitting In —

Dana fit right in, and Border was glad to have her there and he could tell his father was too. She wasn't his kid of course, but they'd all been together so long that those sorts of details got dim.

Dad, she called the old man, just like Border did.

The first two days, the phone was buzzing with calls between Red Cedar and Santa Fe. Border only heard Dana's side:

"I'm eighteen, I'm out of school, I'm a free woman, you can't make me, I'm staying."

Border took the phone during one argument, told her he missed her, then said, "Back off, Mom."

That felt good.

On Saturday Liz and Jacob came over to meet Dana, and Border could tell right away that Jacob was hooked, bad. "Quit panting," he whispered to him.

Dana brought out notebooks that were filled with poems she'd written on the bus rides between food factories. "I've been dying to read these," she said, "and now I have an audience." Jacob settled in, Border groaned, Liz remembered chores at home.

"Get your recorder and play," ordered Dana. Border glared at his sister.

Liz said maybe she would stay, the chores could wait. "We've never heard him play. Is he good?"

"A maestro. Play while I read, Border. These poems need music."

"I'm rusty."

"You'll be fine. Play that song you do by Boiled in Lead."

"Dana, I don't want to."

The old man appeared. "I'm going for groceries."

"I'll come and help," said Border.

"I'm probably needed at home," said Liz.

Dana and Jacob stayed behind, getting acquainted.

Shopping —

Shopping with his father was like shopping with Connie — the old man was too busy talking to be of any help. Border pushed ahead with the cart, filling it with stuff his father would never buy. Maybe he'd notice at the checkout, but then it would be too late.

Fudge Mania or Pralines n' Chocolate? Border mulled, decided to get both.

"Is that how you got so tall, eating ice cream?"

Border turned around, smiled at a man.

"Like father, like son."

Where was his father? Border looked around, saw a store full of strangers.

This one was chatty. "I once saw your dad eat a whole Lollapalooza sundae — fifteen scoops of ice cream, three toppings. He ever tell you about that?"

"No."

"Probably not. He was under the influence, you might say. Talk about having the munchies! Back then your dad sure lived on a different planet. A walking drugstore, old Gumbo."

Border pushed the cart along. The man followed. "Never figured Gumbo Baker would survive the sixties, what with all the junk he put in his body."

Border glanced at the stranger, noted the plump hands holding several frozen pies.

"When I heard he'd gone to Canada, I figured it was a mistake. Guessed he meant to go to Mexico, score some dope, but he was so messed up he went the wrong way."

Border stopped the cart, gripped the handle. "I'm not really interested, sir."

"I was in 'Nam when I heard about him taking off to Canada. Serving my country. I couldn't believe it when I found out he came back. We don't want him here."

"Look, mister, he's over in aisle two or some place. Maybe the deli. Go tell him, okay?"

"Smart-ass, aren't you?"

Did he dare? Yeah, why not. "Better than being a dumbass." He rolled the cart away, double-time, picturing the headline in the local paper.

Pies hurled at Border.

He saw the man again in produce, talking angrily to a woman. Border eyed them while selecting oranges, stood straight when he saw the woman raise her arm and whack the man in his gut with celery. She wheeled her cart around and pushed it toward Border.

He wished he were at the house, even if it meant listening to his sister's poems and watching Jacob fall in love. Anything would be better.

The woman confronted Border. "That guy's a jerk," she said.

"He doesn't seem to like my dad."

"Don't believe anything he said to you. His opinion is nothing, worse than nothing. Your dad was the sweetest guy, the best guy. If I'd been smart and been interested in him instead of the losers I did go with in high school, then maybe my life wouldn't have been so messed up."

Border was bumped from behind. He turned and smiled at a toddler pushing a toy cart. He headed toward the potatoes. The woman followed.

"He was nice to me when no one else was."

"That's good." Five pounds or ten? Dana loved 'em mashed; better get ten.

"Not interested in talking about him, I guess. Can't really blame you. Probably been hearing plenty about good old Gumbo since you came to town."

"That's true."

"And I've heard plenty about you."

Border lifted a banana bunch. Too green?

"I've heard that you're quite the little patriot."

"What?"

She moved her cart, making way for an elderly couple

pushing through the aisle. "Someone told me that last week you were with all the folks at Christ Fellowship, packing up boxes for the soldiers."

This town. Suspected he couldn't pee without it being reported.

"I went to help friends."

"The old ladies loved you, that's what I heard. Someone said — Oh my gosh, Gumbo!"

Border stepped back as his father joined them. The two adults grinned at each other.

"Wow, Maggie, you look great. Last time I saw you, you were . . . oh, I don't know . . ."

Border looked around, spotted twenty or thirty carts between the potato bin and freedom. Should he make a break?

"I was seventeen and pregnant and about to be run out of town. Would you believe it, Gumbo, now I'm a grandmother!"

"Dad, the ice cream's gonna melt. We should go."

"Are you living in town, Maggie?"

"Since November. My mom died and Dad got sick and then he decided maybe I wasn't so evil. I finally felt I could come back. I'm a secretary for some lawyers. It's okay."

"Married?"

"Divorced. Again."

"At least give me the checkbook, Dad. I'll go pay."

"Maggie, your story sounds like mine. Buy you a drink sometime and let's talk."

"Make it coffee."

If he screamed, would he be heard?

"Make it dinner. When?"

Border lifted his father's hand and clamped it onto the shopping cart handle. "You're in charge, Dad."

102

He walked away, dodging carts and shoppers. Headed home on foot.

Walking —

In Albuquerque last summer, Border had once walked all night. It was the first cool evening after four deadly hot days and nights. His father was due at the hospital early the next morning and had gone to bed. Border didn't want to go to bed, so he'd gone out for a candy bar at the store around the corner, but before he got there he saw cop cars and ambulances a few blocks away. The flashing lights and gathered crowd attracted him, so he went that much farther.

There was a death, one so fresh that the covered body was only just disappearing into an ambulance as Border approached.

The sight dazed him. A death, a dead body. Just a boy, people were saying. Border didn't want to see any more, so he kept on walking.

The street was busy with cruisers — an endless stream of cars loaded with kids, who were loaded with beer, or other stuff. In the parking lot of the store where he finally stopped for the candy bar, there was a fight — not too serious, just pushing and shoving, creative name-calling. Border came out of the store and didn't respond to a taunt that spilled over from the fight to him. Three boys piled into a car and followed. Too far from home, no bus in sight, what could he do?

Border hurried up. Things whizzed by his head as the boys followed, shouting and jeering from the car. He felt something hit above his ear, reached and pressed gum into his long hair. He touched it for only an instant, but he could feel it smear and spread, soft gum, still wet with saliva. He knew it was stuck and he'd have to cut it out. Cut the hair short; the gum was mashed to the roots. Okay, he'd shave it, but only that side.

Eleven P.M. Any barbershops open?

Something heavier whizzed by on his left and he turned to the right, following a side street. The car came too, brakes squealing as it made the turn. Up ahead, the street rose, crossing over an arroyo. Border speeded up, so did the car, then he ran down the slope, skidding and slipping on gravel, catching himself, scraping his hand. He hopped over boulders and landed on concrete. The car roared by overhead, while Border caught his breath.

Maybe they'd be too lazy to get out of the car and follow him into the drainage ditch. He could hope, but he better keep moving.

The arroyo was flat on the bottom, wide as a sidewalk, with high sloped walls. Border's feet scraped along dry concrete. There'd been no rain for days, but he knew even the shortest shower could fill it up with a dangerous current. A bad place to fall asleep.

Keep moving, Border.

He turned right and went south. The arroyos channeled water all the way to the Rio Grande, on the other side of the city. Could he walk that far?

Midnight, his feet started hurting. Stopped and sat. A spotlight from someone's back yard shone down, then went off. Bedtime. He hoped his father was still sleeping.

Hard to see with no light. Right in front of his face his hands were black patches. He moved them around, shadowy contortions.

104

One A.M., walking along, not sure where he'd be if he climbed to the street. He stumbled over trash. It was hard to see.

"Hey fella," said a voice, "got a dollar?"

Border stopped, looked around, and saw a shadow sitting a few feet on down.

"Got a dollar for some coffee?"

Border remembered the change from the five he'd used when he bought the Snickers.

"Just a dollar, you bastard. Just one."

"No money."

"Got a smoke?"

"No."

"Then get out of here. This is my place. You're big but I could still hurt you."

Border believed it and hurried on.

Two A.M. The lights above got bright, a wide yellow haze. He crawled up to the top, slipping once, scraping his hands again. Two blocks away, a cop car cruised through the parking lot of a shopping center. Border knew where he was. Nowhere close to home.

He felt raindrops and decided to stay out of the ditch. Walked along, looked up at the sky, but no more rain wet his face. Puzzled, until he noticed he was near a bank, and a sprinkler was watering grass. The drops made him thirsty. He knew about an all-night restaurant nearby and he headed that way.

Border ordered coffee, his first cup ever, and he made a face when he sipped. As soon as the waitress breezed by, he called out for a Coke, but by the time she brought it he'd gone back to the coffee and finished the cup.

Two older girls sat in the booth behind his. The girl closest to Border turned around and said, "You've got gum in your hair."

"God, that's great hair," said the other. "I could spend forty dollars at the shop and never get a blonde that rich. Is it natural? I bet it is."

The first one kneeled on the bench of her booth, right behind Border. He hadn't said a word, but she picked at the gum with one hand. The other hand rested on his neck.

Border sipped his Coke.

"Can't get it," she finally said. "It's really stuck."

"Thanks for trying," he said, without turning around.

"What else can I do for you?"

He dug money out of his pocket, set it on the table, and left. He could hear the girls laughing.

He walked east toward home, and got there as the sky lightened behind the Sandias. Silhouetted by the sunrise, the mountains resembled a gray slumbering beast hovering over the city.

Just as he crawled into bed his father rose. The light in the hall went on; the bathroom door closed. Whistling in the shower. A new day, get on with it, go to work.

Border slept.

Already? —

His father was home with the groceries by the time Border reached the house. Cold hands, numb feet. Chided himself about buying boots. Do it, just do it, he commanded.

Dana came out with Jacob, and they stood holding hands in the driveway.

Already?

They didn't see Border until he called. Jacob took a step from Dana; their hands slipped apart.

"Where have you been?" his sister asked.

"Walked home from the store. Is Dad angry?"

"Sort of. But not at you."

"At you?"

"The grocery bagger. Eggs were broken. I'm going to Jacob's to meet his family."

Already?

Inside the house, Border kicked off his shoes and leaned over to rub his feet. His socks were wet, and he pulled them off. His toes flamed red.

Sweet Boy —

He recovered his car keys and all privileges. There was no formal declaration; his father just asked him to do an errand the next day, tossed him the keys, and didn't ask for them back. Border resumed driving to school, and he always came home to find Dana on the sofa, watching TV.

"You're not a real good advertisement for early graduation," he commented.

"I have two fathers and don't need a third."

She bestirred herself enough to visit Jacob's house a few times, and often went with Border to the basement of Christ Fellowship.

"The old ladies like *you* almost as much as they like me," said Border one night after they'd been to the church.

"Not so, they like me best."

107

"Me."

"Me."

"Me."

"It *would* be you," said Dana, "if you'd play for them. Why don't you ever play anymore? I never hear you practice."

"Lost interest, I guess." Not the truth, exactly. What the truth was, he didn't know.

Next day, after school he did play, the first time in days. Pulled the recorder out of the case, warmed it up. It was his mother's birthday. Too poor to buy a present, hadn't even sent a card. Guilt roiled his conscience. Dana had sent a gift and offered to add his name, but Border said, Thanks, I'll come up with something.

He loosened up with a few folk songs. She'd never liked rock. Then some Mozart. That stopped him for a moment, thinking, *How many sixteen-year-old guys can blow a rondo?*

He called the lab. Her assistant was snooty; Border was firm. Just get her, okay?

"Happy B-day, Mom. Now sit still. Give me five minutes." He played for that long.

"What a perfect present," she said.

Her voice was rigid. Controlling tears, he guessed. Weird, Mom — you go naked on stage, but darned if you'll cry at the lab. "Give my best to Lee."

"I will. Thank you for that, too. Love you, darling. Miss you."

"See ya, Mom."

Duty done. What a sweet boy.

Dot Tully's great-nephew was killed in the Gulf during the first day of the ground war. For five weeks there had been planes and bombs; now the soldiers and tanks and guns were involved. Border had watched the start of the ground war on television, watched the tape of tanks rolling across the desert, watched the allied armies chase down and overtake exhausted Iraqi soldiers. Like everyone, he knew as he watched that the war was as good as over. Over and won.

He watched everything, cheering them on, unaware of course that someone related to someone he knew was getting killed.

Dot's great-nephew was twenty years old. Border learned that when he showed up at the church the next night. He had two papers to write, but he'd promised to stamp several hundred balloons. They had two rubber stamps he could use: COME HOME SOON and SUPPORT OUR SOLDIERS.

He walked into the church basement and right away saw that something was wrong. No one was working. All eyes were on Dot. Her face was pale, her voice was tight. "He was twenty years old. Just twenty. He was the one who gave Susan, my niece, so much trouble when she nursed him."

All the women nodded, as if they'd actually known.

Dot's great-nephew had never even visited Red Cedar, but people in the church basement decided to have a memorial service for him anyway. Right away, someone said. Before it's all over, before people forget.

"Will you go?" Liz asked Border later, when they were in the kitchen washing up coffee cups.

"Sure. I like Mrs. Tully."

109

"Will it be your first time in church?"

"Yes."

Liz gave him the once-over. Border looked down. Torn jeans, stained shirt, broken shoelaces, mismatched socks.

"Different clothes, huh?"

She plunged her hands into hot water. "I didn't say a thing."

New Clothes —

"Four hundred bucks?"

"The suit I really liked was five."

"You're still growing. I don't spend that much on my suits."

"It shows, Dad."

"Stay out of this, Dana."

"I think he looks great."

"Look at yourself, Border. Who do you think you are? Someone applying for business school?"

"I think I look good."

"He needs a haircut," said Dana, and she rubbed his head with her fist.

"The clerk said I was a perfect size forty."

"You're a perfect something. Four hundred bucks."

"You may as well know, Dad, that the shirt and socks and tie and belt were extra. But I didn't get shoes. My sneakers will do, I think. They're black, after all."

"How much extra?"

"Eighty-five."

"When you asked for the Visa to go shopping, I thought you meant to buy boots."

Border snapped his fingers. "Forgot those."

God and War —

A packed house. Border sat squeezed in the pew between Dana and Liz. He stared at the hair and hats ahead, knew people behind were looking at him. Glad he'd gotten a trim.

Hymns and prayers, sobs from the front where Dot Tully sat. It went on for an hour. The minister hadn't known the soldier so after a few words about the deceased's life, he began to preach about war.

With four hundred bodies, the church heated up. Border felt a little dopey and was glad when the minister finished and the action resumed. Stand up for the singing, bow head for the prayers. Amen here, Amen there. Everyone, even Dana, always seemed to know what to do. Border followed, a beat behind.

"Lovely, lovely," people murmured after the final hymn.

"I need to get out of here," Liz whispered.

"Too hot?" Border asked. "I was feeling a little groggy." He followed her through the slow-moving crowd, out the door and onto the broad front steps. The cold night air jerked him awake.

Liz banged the stair rail. "I cannot believe that he actually used the word 'infidel'."

Border frowned. Infidel? Missed that. Maybe he had fallen asleep.

"I don't understand," she said, "how one human being

111

can stand up in front of other equally intelligent human beings and actually claim that he knows what God is thinking. How can he do that?"

"That's his job."

"Some job."

"You surprise me, Liz."

"Why?"

He shrugged. "I know you're pretty religious —"

"I am, but don't make assumptions. Don't you dare make assumptions about what that means."

Whoa. Oh-kay. Wouldn't think of it. He gestured toward the door. "I thought you liked this. That's my only assumption."

"I love the singing, Border. I love the people. I love to pray. I believe in . . . things. I hate preaching."

"Generally, or just tonight?"

"Generally. The whole idea of it."

"I liked it."

"You were asleep."

Possibly. "I was not. It was my first time, and I enjoyed it. I liked the way everyone knew what to do. When to sing, what to say."

"Auto-pilot religion."

"It didn't feel that way. It felt like . . . belonging. I liked that."

"Sure," Liz said. "You're free to belong. You're welcome. You're not an infidel."

"I think you're being too critical. I think —" He caught himself. Why was he defending her church?

Liz smirked and started to speak — something sharp, with barbs. He could feel it coming.

112

The church door opened and Liz zipped her lips. Border smiled. Saved.

"Sneakin' smokes, kids?"

Border and Liz looked around and stood up straight.

"Hello, Mrs. Zipoti," Liz said. "We're just cooling off." Border remembered two late assignments and sagged in his new suit.

"Too much fire and brimstone, eh? Can't say I disagree. Have you kids met Mr. Zipoti? Probably not. I only let him out once a year." She — alone — enjoyed the joke while Liz and Border acknowledged the man behind her. He paused long enough from his pipe-lighting to nod.

"Liz, you did a wonderful job on that reproduction assignment. This sex unit is a tough one, but it looks like you'll pull off your usual *A*. Border, I don't think I saw a paper from you."

He ran a hand nervously up a four-hundred-dollar lapel. When in doubt, make a joke. "Gosh, Mrs. Zipoti. I didn't think I should write it until I tried it."

Mr. Zipoti laughed, but then sucked air at the wrong moment and took in smoke. Ha ha, hack hack. His wife swatted him on the back. He recovered.

"Thanks, dear. I'd be a dead man without you."

"Glad you admit it." She turned back to Border. He felt the heat of her gaze. Why didn't the snow melt?

"Funny boy, Border, but have it on my desk by Friday, or zero points. Can you afford zero points?"

"No, Mrs. Zipoti."

"Well, then." She slipped her arm through her husband's. "Look at these steps, Caleb. We Methodists are much better at shoveling, don't you think?"

"Yes, Midge."

Liz and Border watched them walk carefully down the steps. "Let's go in," she said, after the couple had walked away. "I don't want to meet any more teachers and I'm done complaining."

Border didn't move.

"My toes are freezing."

Nothing.

"What's the matter? Worried about those zero points? Just write the stupid paper."

"It's not that."

"What?"

God and war? Hymns and prayers? Death and infidels? He'd been full of it five minutes ago, but it had all slipped away. His own toes curled from the cold, while his head rattled with the thought that had stunned him.

"C'mon, Border. What?"

He turned to his friend. "Her name is *Midge?*"

Cease-fire —

The war was over. The announcement came from the president right when the people in Red Cedar were honoring Dot Tully's great-nephew.

Border stayed up late, tuned to the news.

Victory is ours! cried the politicians.

An honorable end, the president said.

Saddam is destroyed, claimed a general.

The next day even more flags and ribbons appeared at school. Border sneaked out during his lunch hour, ran six blocks to the church, found what he wanted in the basement, and returned to school. During study hall, seventh period, a senior he barely knew passed the carrel in the library where Border was working and said, "Cool idea. I'll help." Other students joined in. The librarian heard the noise, caught sight of the mess, came to see. He nodded approval and went away. They all worked for an hour, huffing and puffing till nearly everyone hyperventilated. Then, just before three o'clock, they opened the windows. When the final bell rang, they stuffed, pushed, let go.

Three hundred yellow balloons caught the wind and sailed.

IV

Peace

Boots —

The war was over but winter dragged on. An early March storm dumped ten inches of snow. Connie and Paul got fed up, got in the Cadillac, and left town. Border took in their mail and papers, and shoveled their driveway after the next three storms. Every few days he got a post card from them. St. Louis, Dallas, Houston, New Orleans, Mobile. He pinned the cards up in his room by his bed. He liked to look at them and think about a trip, his own trip. Where would he go, if he could go?

If he could go, would he?

They came back in the middle of the biggest storm. Border was hauling garbage cans down to the curb ("It's Minnesota," his father had said, "and of course they'll pick it up in a blizzard, so would you please just do it?"). He saw the Cadillac drive slowly up the unplowed street. It fish-tailed, then straightened. Snow shot up as Connie accelerated to make the turn into their driveway. Paul waved, then covered his eyes as the car skidded, spun, slid backward into snow. A car door opened. "Hi, hon," Connie called. "We're home." Border got his father and sister and they pushed the car free.

It snowed for one more day and night, and the wind blew

for another day, then it snowed again. When it was calm, Border looked out the window at his driveway, all filled in and hidden by snow. Time at last, he decided, to buy boots.

He had to ask for money, of course. Did it carefully. Cooked a nice meal, did three loads of wash, vacuumed. His father noticed. "What do you want?" he said. "Boots," replied Border. The money was handed over, maybe with some extra thrown in, but Border wasn't sure; he didn't know how much boots cost.

Next day after school he found a shoe store on Main. There weren't too many stores left on the street; they'd all gone to the mall. A florist, a gift shop, one menswear, a sporting goods, three beauty salons, the shoe store. The shoe store was on the block next to the courthouse. Border parked by the banner announcing the memorial. One corner had blown loose and he stopped to retie the cord. A gust of wind snatched it out of his fingers and the nylon rope whipped up, hitting his face. Yow! He touched his cheek. Blood? No, just pain.

The shoe store was deserted except for a clerk, an old man, who sat smoking a cigar. Border nodded and browsed. Not much to see, unless he wanted wingtips.

"I don't carry tennis shoes," the man said. Puff, puff. "You boys only ever want tennis shoes."

"I want boots. Warm ones."

The man rose, looked at Border's feet, then walked to the back of the store. Border inhaled. He liked the cigar smell. Maybe he should take it up. He sat down and leaned back, imagining. Puff, puff.

The man returned and dropped a box at Border's feet. "Try these." He stepped back, crossed his arms. Border got the message: Help yourself.

Beautiful boots, just what he wanted. Leather laces, felt

120

liners, thick rubber soles. He slipped one on and tied it up. Perfect. "You just looked at my foot and knew the size?" he asked the man.

"Yes. Do you want them or not?"

Main Street, the friendly street. Border thought about saying no, debated walking out. Imagined grabbing the cigar and shoving it somewhere. An eyeball? The gut? A wingtip?

He wanted the boots, he said. The man kneeled down, knees cracking, undid the lace with a pull and yanked the boot off. "I'll ring these up."

At the register, Border counted through the tens his father had given him, happy to see two left over after he'd paid. Twenty bucks. He'd make it last.

"How's your father doing?" the man asked, voice as crisp as the bills he was handling.

Border glanced down at his jacket. Had someone pinned a note? *Gumbo's boy.* He touched the back of his head. Maybe the barber had shaved it into his hair. "Dad's fine. He's pretty happy to be back in Red Cedar."

"Some people aren't real happy he's here." The man slammed the register drawer closed, trapping Border's money. "Some people think he should have stayed in Canada."

"He hasn't lived in Canada for over ten years."

A detail, and it didn't matter to the shoe man. He just stared, cigar rolling in his mouth. Puff puff, puff puff.

Seeing Red, Eating Pink —

"I should have walked out of there. I should have dumped the boots on his head. I should at least have yelled at the guy."

"Like you're yelling at us, hon?" Connie asked.

"Sorry. But the guy just burned me, and all I did was smile and hand him forty bucks."

"I gave you sixty," said the old man.

Oops. "Laces were extra, Dad."

"Sure."

"You want it back?"

"No. Consider it compensation for rising to my defense. I appreciate it."

"I didn't rise to anything, that's what's bugging me. And what really steams me, Dad, is how come it's always me that gets the mudslinging? You're the one they're mad at, but I get my butt kicked. All you've gotten is a cake. I'm tired of it. I'm tired of living in this two-bit town where I can't even buy boots without offending someone. Has anyone said anything to you? Once, just once, have you caught crap for what you did?"

"Save it for home, Border. We'll discuss this later."

"Keep going," said Connie. "I think it's interesting."

"C'mon, Dad, what's the worst? Been jumped? Kicked? Hounded in the grocery store? What?"

"Actually, no one has said a thing."

Border swore.

"That's not interesting," said Connie.

"Ha! And *your* mouth is always so elegant?" Border said and wished right away he hadn't.

Paul appeared in the kitchen doorway. "Time to eat. You can fight later, but not over my cooking."

Dana had helped Paul with supper. He needed a hobby for a character in his new book. He'd ruled out bell ringing and hang-gliding and was now considering cooking. He was experimenting with recipes.

"Tomato and basil linguine," Dana announced as they all sat down. "And I warn you, this might be the perfect pasta."

Border looked at his plate and his day went from bad to worse. "Oh, man," he groaned. Pink noodles.

Talk Time —

Border wasn't surprised when his father knocked on the bedroom door that night. Talk time. He supposed he had asked for it.

The old man didn't waste any time. "What you said to Connie was inexcusable."

"I apologized later. Yes, it was wrong."

"I don't ever want you saying anything to Paul or Connie that needs an apology. Ever."

"I don't want to either. Things slip out. They handle it better than you."

"And I'm sorry you've had trouble since we moved to Red Cedar."

Just as he thought, the real subject. Connie was a warm-up. "I'm the new kid in town, Dad. Again. For the millionth time in my life, I'm the new kid in town. Did you ever think about what it would be like for me before you decided to move us?"

"I knew it wouldn't be easy for you."

"Perceptive."

"But I knew I had to get you out of Albuquerque. The house was here and it seemed like the perfect chance to get away. I'm sorry it hasn't been better for you."

"What was so wrong with Albuquerque?"

"Do I really have to tell you? Border, the things you were doing just —"

"*What* was I doing? I wasn't doing drugs, Dad. I wasn't sleeping around, Dad. Tell me, Dad, just what was I doing?"

The old man rose from the bed, stuffed his hands in the pockets of his jeans. "You were slipping away."

"Slipping away? What's that? Some new category of teen-age sin?"

"It was scary, is what it was."

"I don't remember it that way, Dad. I miss it."

"Our memories differ. Good night, Border."

Memory —

I remember meeting Riley in a comic book store. I had ditched school because the weather was nice, and I wanted to be doing something worthwhile. I decided to track down some back issues of *Elfquest*, my favorite comic. I especially wanted to find #8, "Hands of the Symbol Maker." I took the bus down to UNM, figuring the stores around campus might have what I wanted. One place looked promising. A kid was standing by the counter when I asked the clerk about back issues. The clerk said they didn't have any *Elfquest* that old, and right away the kid said, "I know where you can get it. C'mon." I followed him out and down the street. When we passed a restaurant, the kid stopped. "You got any money?" he asked. "Sure," I answered, and we went in and ordered. He was hungry and ordered lots, steak and eggs. I got pie. Other kids came in and talked to him. I learned his name, Riley. Told him mine. A pregnant girl came in, sat next to Riley, laid her head on his shoulder. "Would you get her some food?" he asked. "She's eight months along, she's gotta eat."

I ordered and paid at the counter, returned with more steak and eggs. She only ate toast. Riley finished the rest.

We sat for three hours, talking. No one chased us out of there. Three hours, too much tea. I went to the bathroom. When I returned, they were gone. A napkin was propped against a glass. A note.

Riley and Celeste cordially invite you to a party, Friday night at 308 Nassau, Apt.4. The host's name is Bruno.

I got on a bus to go home. No comic book, but happy. The next day was Friday and now I had something to do.

Present from Connie —

"What should I do about this, hon?" Connie handed Border a letter, then opened the freezer. "You kids have any ice cream? Oh good, Eskimo Pies. I have to sneak ice cream, you know. Paul can't have it."

"He sneaks it, too. Every time he comes over. Don't tell him I told you. What is this?" Border opened the letter.

"That memorial committee wants to honor Vietnam War Gold Star mothers at the groundbreaking ceremony. There are two of us, Midge Zipoti and me."

"Mrs. Zipoti?"

"Uh huh. Her oldest boy, Gregg, was killed in seventy-three, right before the cease-fire, if you can imagine. Midge's older sister is a buddy of mine, and I was playing cards with her at the club the night the family got the news. Déjà vu all over again."

Border read the letter. "This sounds nice. You *should* be honored. Even if it is twenty years later."

"Twenty years and another war later. Somehow I feel kind of used. Like maybe they're including me because it might help them raise money."

"They're including you because it's right."

"Maybe. Where is everybody? Dana's with Jacob, I suppose. They look pretty serious, I must say. Is your dad worried? Does your mom know?"

"Dana's working. It's her first day at the Sav-Mor. I heard her tell you about the job. As for your other questions, Connie, you'll have to ask my parents."

"Huh. And where is your pop? I brought you all something." She pointed to a box by her purse on the counter. "Well, mostly it's for you and him, but Dana'll get a kick out of it."

"Dad's at a meeting. He's been elected president of the hospital nurses' group, and now he's got meetings once a week. You knew that, too."

"Between meetings and Maggie, bet you hardly ever see him."

"You're really fishing for information tonight."

She feigned insult. "Fishing? Kiddo, I don't fish for information." She pressed empty fingers to her lips and inhaled, then exhaled and smiled. "I go digging with a backhoe."

"What's the present?"

"Pictures. Your grandma couldn't bear to throw them out like your grandpa said she had to, so she gave them to me. Forgot I even had them until I went to the basement this afternoon to put away the pasta maker. Eighty bucks and he used it twice. I've gotta go. If I stay any longer, Paul will know I've been eating. Enjoy the present. Good night, hon."

Border saw her out, then picked up the box she'd left and took it to his room.

Pictures, all right. Big ones, little ones, black and white, a few in color. His father was in every one. His father little and chubby, in a striped T-shirt and coonskin hat. His father in a Superman costume, lifting the cape. Holding a BB gun. Smiling, gap-toothed, over a crooked bow tie. Punching a baseball glove. His father taller, no longer chubby, face peppered with pimples. Holding a golf club. Family shots — his uncle, two people he supposed were his grandparents. His dad with Connie and her boys. Picnics. Christmas.

Pictures. Some had been torn. Border fingered a rough edge on one, imagining his grandfather ripping it out of the family album. He found a formal portrait of the family, and studied his grandfather. Tall and bald. Border rubbed his head, hoped it wasn't genetic.

Birthday parties, backyard football. His father and his uncle holding a stringer of fish. Their father standing to the side, so proud.

Did it work for him? Did the outraged housecleaning help him forget? Help him wipe away the memory of his son the draft dodger, his son the traitor. His son the fisherman. On a long winter night, when there was nothing to do but sit in a chair and look out the window, did he ever once think about, remember, miss his son?

Border put the pictures away and set the box on the floor. Lay on his bed and thought, *Did he ever wonder about me?*

"Don't take long, Dana," Border said. "You have to get to work and I have an appointment at Tire Town."

"It'll just be a minute. I want to see if Jacob's feeling better, and I want to give him grief for being sick on my first two days of work."

"You could have called."

"I haven't seen him in three days. Just for a minute."

"Five bucks if it's any longer and fifty cents every minute extra." Border stayed in the car and timed her. The instant the McQuillans' door closed behind her, he began counting the seconds. One, two . . . fifty-eight, fifty-nine, sixty. Kept counting. One minute, two, three. Pew — carbon monoxide. He turned off the ignition. She was slow, he was cold.

Border went to the door, knocked, and walked in. He was greeted by Pooch and little girls, sisters. He was pretty sure it was Pooch who drooled on his hand.

"Where's Dana?" he asked. "She's supposed to be at work in fifteen minutes."

Liz was loading the dishwasher. "She's downstairs with Jacob."

Mrs. McQuillan was on the phone and waved a greeting. "Border Baker just walked in," she said. His name, he could listen. "I'll ask him, Dot. You call the others. If we get an okay from enough regulars, let's just go ahead. I'll check the figures and see what money we have left and get back to you."

Border saw coffee, poured himself a cup.

"Make yourself at home," a sister said.

"Thanks."

"Your hair is weird today," she added.

Border nodded. "Good. That's how I like it." When he'd gotten his last trim, he'd told the barber to shave it on the bottom and let it grow on top. This morning he'd groomed the top into four spikes, all in a row.

"It's like a stegosaurus," she said. Liz whacked her sister's rump with a towel and she ran out of the kitchen.

Mrs. McQuillan hung up the phone and looked sternly at him. "I've noticed," she said, "that you and your sister drink an awful lot of that stuff. I didn't start until I was in college."

"Big-city habit," he said. "Picked it up hanging out in coffee shops."

"It's a habit all right. I picked it up hanging out at church. Border, I need your vote on something. Have you heard about the new war memorial?"

"Sure. And the ceremony and everything. Connie — Mrs. Sanborn — was invited to be part of the dedication."

"It's about time they do something for her. The committee for the memorial is soliciting money for the monument. They've asked all civic groups to contribute, including LICM. Dot Tully and I were just talking, and now that the project is done we thought we'd contribute any leftover money."

"Sounds good."

"That's another yes vote. A few more and we'll go ahead."

"You didn't ask me," said Liz.

"One vote per house. Where's the darn checkbook?" She opened a drawer, pushed around clutter. "Aha, here we go. Calculator? Yes."

Mrs. McQuillan sat at the table punching numbers. Border sat and sipped coffee. Pooch came into the room, turned in a circle, lay down on Border's left foot. Pinned in place, he couldn't hurry away.

One of the little sisters returned. Border always got confused about their names. "Don't you have to get home?" she asked. "Don't you have chores?"

"No, I don't," he answered, and made a face at her. She ran out of the room.

"I don't believe this," Mrs. McQuillan said.

"No money?" Liz asked.

"Worse. We're ninety dollars overdrawn. The bank must have covered it for us, but we'll have to repay. I didn't see a notice from the bank. How did I let this happen?"

"What will you do, Mom? Get people to chip in?"

"We did that at the last meeting. I can't ask for more money. This is my mistake; I didn't watch expenses carefully enough. All that postage. Sure, we said, let's write to a thousand soldiers. Two thousand. Sure, let's buy the balloons. Oh, geez." She lowered her head in her hands and rubbed her forehead.

"We can pay. Ninety bucks won't kill us," said Liz.

"I know that. I'll cover it. The bad part is that the group doesn't have anything to donate to the memorial. People will be disappointed."

Pooch yawned and rolled, pinning the other foot. Border sipped his coffee and helped himself to a donut from a plate on the table. Munched and thought. He had an idea.

New Hat —

First, he needed a hat.

"Where can I buy a hat?" he asked Liz.

"What kind of hat?" He explained, then she asked, "Wouldn't a coffee can do?"

130

"No, I definitely need a hat. It doesn't work without one. I can't work without a hat."

Not until Tuesday did she come up with an answer. She passed him a note in Resources, evading Mrs. Zipoti's predator eye. *Salvation Army thrift shop is open today. Or try Wayne's Western World in Hayfield.*

The thrift store had nothing he could use, so on Wednesday he went to Hayfield. Liz, Dana, and Jacob went along. "A road trip," Border said.

"Not really," said Jacob. "It's only twenty miles."

Right in the middle of Minnesota farm country, a western store. Feed, saddles, bridles, and blankets.

And hats.

He found a perfect one on sale for thirty dollars. A display hat, it had scratched leather and a frayed band, but the style and shape were just what he wanted. He tried it on.

"Border," Liz said. "Your hair!"

"Looks good," said his sister.

When he took it off, the spikes were bending in every direction. "I like it," Border said. "Too bad I only have twenty bucks."

Dana went up to the clerk, who'd been watching them. "Can I help you, girl?" the woman said. Dana ran her hands through her bright green hair, then tugged on a gold loop, not the one in the nose. "Yes, you can, Ma'am. Wow, I like that tattoo." The clerk lifted her hand, rippled her fingers. Border saw a bucking horse move by the knuckles.

Dana explained why they wanted the hat. "And one of the moms that'll be honored is a friend," she said, finishing up. "It's a real good cause."

"Shoot, kids, that's an old hat anyway. Practically every

little kid that's been in the store the last two years has tried it on. You can have it for nothing." She punched at the register and the drawer shot open. She pulled out a bill. "And here's a little seed money. But promise me one thing, boy," she said, looking at Border.

"He promises," said Dana.

"Play a little country. Play a song for me. My name's Arlene."

Town Square —

Border licked his lips. Saturday morning, nine A.M., he should be in bed. Rolled the recorder in his hand. Had he practiced enough?

The manager of the Sav-Mor came by. "It's too cold today for you to stand in the entry. Let's move you over by the deli. Someone get that poster, wouldja? Tape it right over this sale sign."

Dana obeyed, and MUSIC FOR THE MEMORIAL, SPONSORED BY LICM covered up EGG ROLLS, 2 FOR $1.49.

"Son, we're turning off the Muzak, but I gotta warn you that on the half hour, I get on the intercom to announce the manager's specials."

"No problem. We just appreciate everything," Border said.

"It's a good thing, what you're doing. Play away."

Border set down his hat. He pulled Arlene's five-dollar bill out of a pocket and tossed it in. He'd learned long ago that you never start with an empty hat. People don't want to be the first to give. Money only flows if others are giving too.

He calmed himself with deep, even breaths, keeping his eyes on the speckled gray floor. He could tell that people passing by with their carts and lists were looking at him. First song was always the hardest.

It had been so long. It was never easy.

Memory, II —

The very first time I ever set out a hat and played for money, I was thirteen years old. We'd just moved to New Mexico. That time I used a Minnesota Twins baseball cap from 1987, the year they won the World Series. The cap was my dad's, a birthday present from his friend Jeff.

I'd sneaked the cap and sneaked out. Going to the library, I told them. Oh, books, they probably thought; books are good. See you later, son. Neither one noticed I took my recorder.

Did I know what I was doing? Hardly. I barely even knew my way around the UNM campus. It's where my mom was working on a Ph.D. I'd been there to visit her office a few times, and I'd seen and heard guys play guitars for spare change on the campus mall. The seed was planted then, you might say. Blossomed, you might also say, the day my paltry allowance was withheld for mysterious reasons. Okay, not so mysterious: my little accident with a can of soda and the VCR.

Homecoming Saturday, the campus was crawling with parents and other adults. They all had money in their pockets. I found a spot in front of some pampas grass near the student union. I was skinnier and shorter back then. Too cute to think about. I closed my eyes and played. The money flew into the hat.

I might have gotten away with it except I forgot to take

the money out of my jeans and Dad collected clothes for laundry the next day before I was up.

"Where'd this money come from?" he wanted to know.

"You were doing what?" said my mom.

"My autographed Twins hat?" said Dad.

"How much did you make?" asked Dana.

Forty bucks, that time. Not bad.

But I must have sounded pretty bad, though Mom insists I could play beautifully the first time I picked up a recorder. That was in fourth grade, back in Fort Collins. That year they handed out plastic ones, and we practiced for weeks, finally performing "Row, Row, Row Your Boat" for the spring concert. The music teacher gave me a solo, "You Are My Sunshine." I guess it went well, but I only remember being scared. That's when I learned to get through it by closing my eyes and ignoring the world. Shut it all out — my personal secret of success.

Showtime —

Border closed his eyes and played. First song, he was a little stiff, but it was a march, "Stars and Stripes Forever," so it went okay. When he finished, people clapped, and he heard a few coins hit the hat.

Dana was there and she hawked for him. "All donations go to the construction of the county war memorial. Give to the memory of those who gave everything!"

Border opened his eyes. "Shouldn't you be bagging groceries?"

She tied on her store apron. "You're on your own."

134

A grocery store is a noisy place. People come in talking, start banging carts, yell at their kids. The deli was a few yards into the store and by the time people reached Border, they were focused, ready to shop. Rolls, milk, Cheerios, sliced ham . . . hey, what's this?

So many people stopped to listen that the manager came and moved displays to make room. Border played on.

Ten o'clock, he took a break, counted the money. Sixty bucks, not bad. He started putting it in his pocket, but just then Dana came by and said, "Don't do that. If people see you, they'll think you're keeping it." She left a few bills in the hat and took the rest back to the store's office.

Right before noon Mr. and Mrs. McQuillan arrived with two of their girls and a couple of extras, friends of the girls. Border was between songs, drinking juice to cool a parched throat.

"That's the one," the youngest daughter said.

"Weird hair," said one of the extras.

"Looks just like a stegosaurus."

He set the recorder between his lips.

"He's the one who loves my sister."

Huh? Border blew a bad note and lowered his recorder.

"And his sister loves my brother." The girls studied Border. Mrs. McQuillan made an apologetic noise. Her husband grinned. One of the extras opened and closed her mouth. "Sisters and brothers? That's against the law," she announced.

Border resumed playing. The Replacements, "My Little Problem."

Early afternoon, the crowds got heavy, and money filled the hat. He finished a song and opened his eyes. Connie was

135

right in front. She didn't say a word, but set down a bill and turned to go.

A fifty. "Connie, no!" he called. "Take it back." She didn't stop, just waved him off as she wiped away tears.

Two o'clock, he was dead, playing on automatic, playing the simplest music he could remember. When he got the tenth request for "Amazing Grace," he knew he'd have to quit.

Then Arlene from Wayne's Western World came in. "Well, it's true. My husband said I was a fool, but I said no, those kids were for real. How about my country tune?" Border thought for a moment. Country, he was weak on that. But he had one.

Four bars into "Stand By Your Man" he had to open his eyes when he heard Arlene whoop.

"How'd he know that was my song?" She grabbed the girl next to her (Border hoped it was her daughter) and danced a little.

By three o'clock he'd seen everyone he knew, including his dad, who was shopping with Maggie. Kids from school, teachers, his barber, even the shoe man.

He quit at four, packing up his recorder to applause.

In the office, Dana helped him count the money. As the figure grew, he sat back and let her count.

Dana finished and looked at him, too stunned to smile. "I guess this is probably your best day ever," she said.

Jacob came in, pulling off his bagger's apron. "How much?"

The manager joined them. "Counted it up?"

"Five hundred dollars," said Border.

"Five-seventeen," said his sister.

Jacob whistled, the manager giggled. "Boy oh boy, son, if

you can bag groceries half as well as you play, you've got a job here."

Border pushed all the money into the hat. "Jacob, give this to your mom, okay?"

"Keep some, Border. No one would mind."

"No."

"At least take minimum wage. More. Take a hundred. Take fifty. Something."

"Give it to your mom."

Jacob protested, Dana said, "Let's go out and celebrate," the manager again offered a job.

"I'm tired," said Border. "I need to nap. But one thing, Jacob."

"Sure."

"I want the hat back."

Phone Call –

He slept for three hours, woke up to an empty house and notes from his dad and sister.

Dinner with Maggie. Again. Border smiled, remembering how Maggie had come to his defense with celery. Decided he was happy for the old man.

Come to the McQuillans. We're playing hearts.

With how many sisters? Not tonight.

He'd spent the day in a grocery store and hadn't eaten a thing. His stomach rumbled, commanding action. He made a six-egg omelet. Wolfed it down, then drank lots of milk straight out of the container. Home alone, why not.

Five hundred and seventeen dollars. Hard not to think

137

about it. Five-seventeen, and just gave it away. Of course he'd only made that much because people were happy to give to the memorial fund. On his own, what would he make?

Begging, Jacob had said.

Better than bagging groceries. If he could just figure out where to play. Courthouse lawn? Probably not, Main Street was dead. Back at the Sav-Mor? Without a cause, he'd get kicked out fast. No begging here, kid.

Almost seven hours of music. What a marathon. Stupid, really, to keep going that long. But he'd done it. He'd played and he'd played. After all, LICM needed the money.

His fingers tapped out the melodic muddle running through his head. Brahms and the Jayhawks. Strauss and the Pixies. Border smiled. Maybe Dana was right: He had needed the music.

The phone rang and he rose slowly. Egg crumbs fell to the floor, got squashed underfoot.

"A collect call from Stephen Riley. Do you accept the charges?"

Mental Rolodex flipped. Stephen Riley? Who?

The electronic operator repeated, "Do you accept the charges?"

Stephen . . . ? Then, it clicked, almost too late. "Yes, I do. Wow, Riley!"

A ten-minute conversation, he hardly got a word in.

"Sorry to call collect, but you know, man, no one has a phone. Dayton's got disconnected, and well, these pay ones need quarters. How you been? Lord, you leave for Minnesota, you fall off the earth. I was up there once, fishing or something with grandparents, and the mosquitoes were terrible."

"How is everyone? I miss Albuquerque."

"That's the thing, you know. Not so good. Weber got busted. The cops stopped him and found two joints in his pocket. He's only fifteen, so they couldn't be too tough; they hadn't done the bust right anyway, but his dad freaked and roughed him up. He took off. I see him now and then, but he's too scared to show up very often because people are looking for him so they can send him back to get beat up again."

"How's Celeste?"

"You know what they did? They took her baby. She lost her baby, man. She'd moved in with this guy who was using, and her caseworker freaked, and out of the blue this other guy shows up and says he's the father, says his parents want the baby. Celeste was so shook up by everyone telling her what to do, she just gave in. Now she has to go to Santa Fe to see it. They've got this big place up there, they're rich artists, you know the type. It's a crime that she's gotta go begging at their door to see her own baby."

"How's the burnt kid?"

"He's around. Never talks. Not a word, ever. It's weird. And he always wears gloves."

"What about you?"

"Okay, I guess. I'm busing dishes at the Frontier a couple days a week. My parents are busting my butt 'cause I don't go to school the way they'd like. What's the point, right? What I was thinking is, we miss you. We were sitting around today wishing that you would come back. On your own. You're sixteen, right? If you did, some of us could get an apartment, then everyone would have a place to go. You could put out the hat and play, I'd bus dishes, Celeste . . . well, if she had a regular place, then she could get the kid back, then she'd start getting checks again. It would work."

"I never thought about doing anything like that."

"Think about it."

"I will. What about the others, are they okay?"

"They're around. Maybe not Patch so much. He was in rehab for a month, now he stays close to home. But Winky is here, he'd be in on it, too. The apartment, I mean. You will think about what I was saying, right?"

Border said he would. He wrote down Riley's address, promised to write, said good-bye.

He hung up the phone and leaned against the wall, digesting eggs and news. The light overhead started buzzing. Fizz, spat — it went out. He stood there in the dark. Celeste and her baby, split up. Weber busted and roughed up. The burnt kid freaked. Patch shipped to rehab.

Come on back, he heard Riley say. Let's get a place.

His friends, Albuquerque. All slipping away.

Money —

Money was a problem. Not in the way that it was for lots of people in the world, of course. Border only had to ask his father and he'd get it. Or some of it. Or write his mother. But he hated to ask for money, and he hadn't *had* to ask for much since he started performing on the streets. He liked earning his own. No strings attached.

He couldn't get it out of his mind: five-seventeen at the Sav-Mor. Play, and they will pay. It had always worked in New Mexico, why not Minnesota?

"You've got to be kidding," Jacob said when Border told him what he was thinking. "Maybe in a big city, but not around here."

"It worked at the store."

"For a cause, Border."

"Where's the nearest big city?"

"Hundred miles north. Get a job, Border. Tie on an apron and work like the rest of us."

Three times a week, Jacob and Dana tied on aprons and bagged at the Sav-Mor. Liz baby-sat and walked dogs for her money. Other kids he knew did other jobs, usually involving fries and hamburgers. Two girls in his math class shelved books at the library; a boy in history sold tickets at the movie theater.

Border could do all that, if he wanted.

He wanted to play. Wanted to set out the hat, offer music, let the cash fall at his feet. Wanted to do what he did best. He hatched a plan.

The Plan, Executed —

Border got lost in Minneapolis trying to find the University of Minnesota campus. The route on the map looked simple enough, but it hadn't mentioned anything about delays due to construction. Or the accident that forced a detour. One-way streets. Dead ends. Signal repairs that backed up cars at intersections.

A new city, things to see, but he kept his eyes on bumpers and road signs. Clock ticked away, using up time. Home by four, that was his plan. He hadn't told anyone what he was doing, just said to his dad, "I feel sort of sick today, think I might throw up. Can I stay home?"

"Throw up? Okay, I guess. I'll call you from work."

"No, don't!"

The old man got suspicious.

"I want to sleep. That's what I need, sleep. The machine will be on."

Lucky — Dana was working all day, extra hours, saving at last for college. Also lucky — she was on a fitness kick, biking to work, wouldn't need the car. He figured he had until four at the latest to be back home.

Once he was near campus he couldn't find parking. Every lot was crammed, and the attendants waved him away. He circled the blocks, hoping.

"Try the city ramp," one attendant said, when Border stopped a second time to plead for admittance. The extra driving around the city, the idling in traffic, the circling for parking all drank up gas, and the gauge needle floated right above empty when he entered the ramp. Half a tank to get back to Red Cedar — eight, nine bucks at least. No problem; soon he'd have money.

He pulled a ticket out of the machine, then noticed the charges. One-fifty an hour.

No problem; soon he'd have money.

Others were walking down the parking ramp and Border followed on foot. Everyone headed toward a cluster of or- ange brick buildings. Bicycles, in-line skaters, streams of kids with backpacks. Border's spirits lifted. A campus. Already he could hear the music, hear the coins. He felt at home.

Past orange brick on to a wide open space. A perfect spring day, and everyone was taking time between classes, filling the chairs, crowding the tables. Two bare-chested guys played Frisbee. A coffee cart was doing good business. Border got in line and thought about Mrs. McQuillan, as he ordered a large cup of Sumatran Royal.

Border looked around, wondering where to set up. Not too close to the tables, he'd irritate people who were trying to study. But too far away, no one could hear. On the far side of the plaza there was a long bridge that led . . . where? More buildings at the far end. He'd heard it was a big school, and from here it seemed to go on forever.

Border walked onto the bridge and got bumped by people who needed to get somewhere fast. Under the bridge, a river, the Mississippi, its fast current churning up caramel-colored froth. Border wondered if anything actually lived in the water. Probably three-eyed fish that glowed in the dark.

Border backtracked and picked a spot where the bridge widened onto the plaza, not far from the chairs, upwind so the sound would carry. He set down his coffee, put out the hat, opened the recorder case. Fished in a pocket and pulled out three ones and a five. All that he had in the world. Set the ones in the hat. Played a few notes, went to work. Smiles, some applause, a few requests.

One request, not so nice: Pack it up, punk; I've gotta study.

At eleven-thirty he counted the money he'd made. Three-twenty. Mostly quarters and dimes. Keep playing, he needed more.

He lost the sun at noon. A few students stayed, braving the gray, but most people packed up and moved inside. April in Minnesota, he decided, is only warm if the sun shines. Border kept playing. Applause from the stalwarts, a few quarters more. Twelve-thirty, almost everyone had disappeared and those that remained outside walked past quickly, heads down. He dug out his gloves, the ones with no fingertips. They helped; still, he was stiff and missed notes.

A bum came by and lunged for the change in the hat. Border was quicker, but not by much. The bum growled, spat on the ground. Walked a few steps away, sat down, started to shout gibberish.

Louder than Border. What could he do?

Border gave up. Time to head home. A final count: four-eighty, plus his own eight bucks. His stomach knotted, and he shivered in the wind. He didn't have enough to get home.

He closed his eyes and wished himself back to Albuquerque, where it was sunny and warm. Where people knew how to fill a hat.

He went into a building to use a bathroom, then sat for a while in a coffee shop. No need to hurry now because he would run out of gas and never get there anyway. He browsed through the school paper. Concerts and sports and tuition hikes. Tomorrow's headline: *Campus musician found frozen in car.*

At the parking ramp he was tempted to drive straight through the wooden arm. Bust out, speed away, beat the cops.

APB: 1984 blue Volvo. Suspect is a male stegosaurus.

"Four-fifty," said the attendant. Border paid the fee.

At the gas station he watched the pump numbers click and the total roll up. His stomach growled. Nothing to eat since breakfast, but he had no money for food. Next time he'd pack a lunch.

Next time?

He started the car, begging the gauge needle to go up. It did, to just under half-full. His spirits shot up. Close enough. He might get home.

Twenty miles, the needle dropped to a third-full.

Fifty miles, it fell to under a quarter tank.

"Lousy mileage!" he shouted. Time for a tune-up.

Seventy miles, the needle started bouncing on orange.

Three miles north of Red Cedar, he ran out of gas. The car coasted onto the gravel shoulder, burped, and died. Border checked his watch. Three-thirty. "This could still work," he said to himself. "I can hike home, bum some money from Dana, find Jacob, and come back with gas. The old man will never know." He locked the car doors and started walking.

One mile, it started to rain. Two miles, a hard wind. He tried his thumb, hitchhiking. A pickup slowed, eased over, then accelerated just before hitting a puddle.

Deluge on Border.

At the edge of town, he passed a gas station. Stupid, he should have saved a quarter for the phone. Never mind. He'd come this far, why bother to call?

When he got home he saw his father standing at the window, looking out, probably watching for him.

Then the door opened and there stood the old man, looking like a general for once in his life.

"Where have you been? Where's the car? Okay, Border, this had better be good."

Border stepped around him into shelter.

"Border?"

Dana was there. She made a slashing move across her throat and left the room.

"This better be good."

Rain and wind, traffic and road construction. The chug, chug, sputter, then silent glide of a dying car.

Border kicked off his shoes. Mud fell onto the floor. Water

145

slid off his hair down his neck. "Oh, Dad," he said. "It wasn't good at all."

Working —

Was this the old lady who liked her eggs packed on the bottom? Border thought so, started to bag with the eggs.

"What are you doing?"

Wrong lady. Started again, left the eggs for the top. She growled her thanks when he finished and lifted the bag into her arms.

Jenny, the cashier, clucked her tongue. "She'll probably go straight to Mr. Pierce and complain."

"Some people like the eggs on the bottom. It's more stable. Hello, sir," he said to the next customer. "Plastic or paper?"

Soup, soup, cat food, soup. After five weeks at the Sav-Mor, Border had achieved bagging perfection. Forty seconds — no more — for an exquisitely loaded grocery bag, tip- and rip-proof. Something to be proud of.

Corn, peas, salsa, tuna. Like the dwarfs, he whistled while he worked. Always his goal to finish the bags before Jenny handed over the receipt. Nice to have goals in life.

He finished at five and picked up his check in the office. He frowned as usual when he saw the amount. "Street musicians," he said to his sister, who was looking at hers, "don't have withholding."

"Go ahead," she said. "Quit your job. Drive to Minneapolis. Earn a fortune. Gosh, little brother, I forget, how did you get home the last time?"

Funny.

"Can I get a ride?" Jacob said.

146

"Aren't you working till six?"

"I begged off. Mr. Pierce let me go. It's kind of slow for a Saturday."

"Too nice outside. People are doing fun things."

"Let's get pizza," said Dana. "My treat."

"Great," said Border.

"I was talking to Jacob. You can come, but I'm not treating you."

"Let's pick up Liz," said Jacob. "She's been baby-sitting all day, but she's probably home now. And how about if we all treat the person on our left?"

"Fine," said Border. "But no pizza. Let's go to that new Chinese place."

"How about Italian?"

"I wouldn't mind red meat."

"Ugh."

"Subs, and let's picnic somewhere."

"Saturday night in Red Cedar," said Jacob. "Who said it couldn't be fun?"

Pooch —

The windows of Jacob's house were dark. "Mom and Dad and the girls are shopping in Rochester," he said. "Liz should be home soon."

A quiet house. What was different?

"Pooch," Jacob called. "Time to go out. Do your thing, Pooch!"

No woofing and howling, no seventy-pound barrel of dog bursting out of anywhere.

"Pooch?"

147

Liz appeared in the basement doorway. "Jacob, come here."

They all followed her down the steps. She switched on a light. Pooch was lying on her doggie bed in the corner.

"I got home an hour ago and she didn't come when I called. I found her here."

"Is she sick?" Border asked.

"She's dead," said Liz.

They all sat down by the dog. Border touched her. Cold. Stiff and cold.

Dana tucked her hands under her arms.

"She must have been dead all day," said Liz. "All day alone, dead."

Jacob hadn't said a word, hadn't touched the dog. Just stared.

"Call the vet," said Border. "They know what to do."

"No," whispered Jacob. He turned to Border, eyes narrowed. "You know what they do? They call a garbage truck."

Liz and Dana made noises.

"I got Pooch for my sixth birthday," said Jacob. "She's not going out in a garbage truck."

"They can cremate, can't they?"

"She's not getting burned up."

"Okay, we'll find a pet cemetery," said Border. "I'll go upstairs and call."

"I don't think so," said Liz. "Our neighbor paid hundreds for her dog's plot. And it was a small dog. Mom and Dad were amazed. They'd never pay."

"Then check with the vet," said Border.

"I know what they do," said Jacob, "and they aren't doing it to my dog. Pooch gets a grave. I'll dig it myself."

"We'll help," said Dana.

"If Mom and Dad get home first," said Liz, "they'll call the vet. We'd better hurry up."

"Besides," Border whispered to his sister, "she might start to smell."

Last Ride —

Put that other bag over her head. Is it tied? Get the shovels. We only have two. We'll stop at our house, I think we have one. Geez she's heavy. Dead weight. Don't joke. Take her rubber duck, she loved that. Does rubber decompose? Watch it, I hit the table. Sorry. I've got the heavy end. She's slipping. This plastic is hard to hold onto. We should've used those bags with handles. Let me do this alone, just get the doors. Keys, please. Not in the trunk! Pooch always loved car rides. Who's got the shovels? Can I put *those* in the trunk? I'll sit with Pooch. She loved it with the windows down. Roll down the windows, it's her last ride, after all. Take her out of the bag, why don't you, and prop her head up in the window. Cut it out, this is sad. This is *weird*. Don't turn so fast, she's sliding off the seat. Hold on. I am, but the bag's ripping. Oh gosh I see an eye. Is that what you call a rolling stop? Don't do anything to attract a cop. Is this illegal? Oh gosh I see a paw. There's Connie. Maybe she won't see us. Fat chance. Everybody wave. Don't come over, please don't come over. She's coming. Forget the shovel, back up. Everybody wave again. Where are we going?

—∾—

"Preserve your pets at Porter's Park Preserve," said Border. He laughed alone. He said it under his breath three times fast, lips moving slightly.

"Stop it now," Dana hissed. "This is not a joke."

The parking lot of the preserve was empty.

"No one else here — that's lucky," said Border. "I don't know how we'd explain what's in the bag if anyone saw us."

"It's getting dark," said Jacob. "Let's get started."

"Now wait," said Border. "I don't want to seem insensitive —"

"You don't seem," said Dana. "You are."

"It's just that I don't want to walk around with a dead dog on my shoulders while we look for a place to bury her. Let's find it first, then I'll come back for Pooch while you guys start digging. Okay?"

"Good idea," said Jacob.

"Okay," said Liz, "but lock the car doors."

Jacob thought the forest trail would be best, but Liz wanted the prairie land. Border flipped a coin and prairie won. They followed a trail for a quarter mile, then started walking over grass. "The creek is this way," said Liz.

"That's good," said Jacob. "Pooch loved water."

Fifteen minutes through grass and mud. The ground got even soggier when they reached a grove of trees and bushes. "This might work," said Border.

"Too close to the trail," said Liz. The others agreed. They kept on walking. More grassland, more mud.

Another grove. When they sat and rested on a fallen tree,

150

they could hear water. "This is it," said Jacob. His sister nodded.

"Are you sure?" asked Border. "Are you sure you won't change your mind and move while I'm getting the dog? It's pretty dark, and I have to be able to find you."

"This is it. This is a good spot. I owe you, Border."

"Yes, you do, Jacob. Supper, at least. And I pick Chinese."

Border was strong, but hiking off-trail with a stiff, dead dog on his shoulders was hard to do. He rested often, which slowed him down, and he fell once, tripping over a stump. His right arm slid into mud up to the elbow. When he got up, he wasn't sure which way to go, so for a while he was certain he was walking in circles.

He heard voices and headed toward them. Hoped it was his friends, but he knew it could be anyone. A Saturday night party under the stars; who's bringing the beer? He thought how freaked the partygoers would be when he stumbled in, mud-covered, dead dog on his back.

Madman of Porter's Preserve. He'd be a legend.

"Border, over here!" Liz's voice reached out and grabbed him. He stumbled again. Under his hand the plastic stretched, pulled, ripped open. Pooch slid out.

"Sorry," said Border, "but I'm tired."

They had dug a hole several feet from the stream. Pooch fit perfectly.

"Hope it's deep enough," said Border.

"We hit rock," said Liz. "It will have to do."

Liz started shoveling in dirt. "Wait," said Jacob. And he pulled the duck from his jacket pocket. "I don't care if it doesn't decompose. Pooch loved this duck."

151

Dana slipped her arm through his. He tossed the toy into the hole.

No one talked on the way back to the car. Dana and Jacob walked quickly and were out of sight when Liz and Border arrived.

"Think they're gone for good?" he asked.

"My brother is lazy. He won't walk home." They stowed the shovels and bags in the trunk.

"What will you tell your parents?"

"I have no idea."

"They won't make us dig her up, will they?"

"I doubt it. We'll just say we buried her somewhere. They probably won't want to know more. Want to go climb the rock?"

"Red Cedar's mountain? No thanks. I'm kind of tired." They walked that way anyway, strolling slowly in the dark. They bumped, then each stepped away. Liz stopped. He turned around and looked at her.

"Border Baker," she said, "you really are different."

"My hair, right?"

"I want to tell you I appreciate the fact that, well . . . most guys would take this opportunity to make a move on a girl. I mean they'd go ahead and assume it would be welcome. Not you."

He slid his hands into his back pockets. "Sounds like you've got some experience."

"You know what else? It just bugs me when people see a guy and a girl together and leap to conclusions."

"Who's been doing that?"

"Girlfriends."

"And sisters?"

152

"Especially them. Wait — have they said anything to you?"

"Not really. I think maybe you give me too much credit, Liz. I am perfectly capable of making a move on a girl. It just hadn't occurred to me."

"Hey — don't hurt my self-esteem!" They both laughed.

"When I came to town," said Border, "I didn't know anyone. And these past few months I think I've just needed a friend more than a girlfriend."

"You don't have to explain. I told you I appreciated it."

"So did I crush the self-esteem?"

"It's just fine, thanks."

They reached the boulder. Liz ran her hands over the letters on the metal plaque. "Do you still feel like you don't belong?"

Border heard sounds from nearby — Jacob, maybe swallowing sobs, Dana's soft voice.

She tapped his shoulder. "Still think you're a glacial erratic?"

"I'm erratic all right."

She turned and leaned against the rock. "If you don't belong here, then where?"

Good question. In Red Cedar, bagging groceries and burying dogs? Or in Albuquerque with his friends, supporting a baby?

Something itched, and Border rubbed his chin. Dried mud crumbled off his fingers. "The only place I belong," he said, "is in the shower."

~⚬~

Did he smell? Dead dog, sweat, and mud — no way he couldn't. All during dinner (where he devoured his chun gar fook and most of his sister's lemon chicken) he imagined that other diners were sniffing suspiciously.

When Border got home he took a hot shower. He stood under the stream until the water wasn't hot, then he dried and dressed fast, racing the chill.

Straight to bed; he was tired. Would he dream about dogs?

Knock, knock.

"I'm asleep," Border shouted. "Go away."

The old man opened the door. "Sorry," he said. "I saw your light go off when I drove up. Hadn't seen you all day and I wanted to say hello. Where were you guys tonight?"

"At the preserve with Jacob and Liz."

"It's nice out there."

"Uh huh."

"Son . . ."

Son? Oh-oh. Talk time.

His father switched on the light and held out the box of photos. "Where did these come from? And I wasn't snooping, so don't accuse me of it. I was collecting laundry this afternoon and found the box under your bed."

"I totally forgot. I'm sorry. Connie brought them over a few weeks ago. They belonged to your parents, I guess, and she kept them after they didn't want them anymore."

"Oh." He sat on the bed.

Border pulled up his legs to make room. "You were pretty cute when you were little."

The old man opened the box, pulled out a photo. "This is me."

"I could tell. That's Uncle Brad, right? And that's Jeff, and his brother, I bet. You know what's funny — Connie had weird hair even back then. Actually, you all had weird hair."

"You're the expert. Look at this one — my tenth birthday. I got that gun for my tenth birthday."

"Striped shirts were really popular in the fifties, I guess."

"Davy Crockett hats."

"You had a potbelly, Dad."

"Whoa, look at this — I had no teeth."

"These are your parents, right?"

"Yep. Looks like a happy family, doesn't it?"

"I bet you were."

"Mostly. Usually. Here's a good one — Brad's graduation from law school. This was taken about six months before I left. Last time we were all together."

"Were you surprised how angry your dad was when you went to Canada?"

"Not at all. I knew he'd be furious. We'd been arguing about the war for months. It didn't matter. I had to leave. I knew he'd be outraged, but I hoped one day he'd calm down. Hoped one day he'd be willing to talk."

"Never did talk, right?"

"Never. One day he died. End of story."

"No regrets?"

"Not about what I did. I avoided Vietnam and found your mother. And Dana. Then we had you." Voice dropped to a whisper. "Best thing I ever did."

"Don't get maudlin, Dad."

"I'd better leave then."

"Sorry about the photos. I did mean to give them to you. Can I have a few? This one would be cool."

"Yuk. It's the worst one. That was taken for my confirmation. Ninth grade, right about when I hit six feet. I couldn't have weighed more than a hundred pounds. And just look at my face. What a mess."

"That's why I like it."

His father closed the box and rose from the bed. "One more thing, Border. I haven't said this in a long time, but now I have to."

More mush, he could feel it coming. Covered his head with a pillow.

"Clean your room."

Alone again. He tacked the photo of his father on the wall, by Connie and Paul's post card from Dallas. It really was an awful picture — goofy grin, gangly body, pimpled face, tight white pants, tight white shirt. An inspiration. A beacon of hope. After all, these days the old man wasn't that bad-looking. For an old man.

Things change.

V

Hometown

Memorial Day —

Suit and tie, white shirt, new sneakers.

"You're going like that?" said his father.

"The shoes, right? Do you think I should wear my old black ones?"

"It's a holiday, Border, and there's a picnic later. Get rid of the tie, at least."

"Maybe *you* should wear it. You have to get on stage when you hand over that check."

"I refuse to wear a tie on a holiday. Dana, let's go, it's late! Where's the check?"

"You put it behind the sofa." Border lifted a large rectangular piece of cardboard and turned it around. "Hospital Nurses Association, Crosby Baker, president. Wow, two thousand bucks!"

"Wasn't my idea. I wanted to give the money to the battered women's shelter. Dana, hurry up!"

They had to park several blocks away from the courthouse, and the crowd there was already so heavy that the three were quickly separated. Border used his height to look around and used his size to edge toward the front. There was a stage on the lawn, with two rows of chairs. Connie and Mrs. Zipoti

159

were in the front row. The Gold Star moms, guests of honor. Connie saw him and waved both hands. Mrs. Zipoti looked stern. Border saw his dad climb to the stage and sit with other people who were holding big fake checks. Mrs. McQuillan saw Border and lifted her cardboard to give it a shake.

Loudspeakers crackled and the speeches began. Connie and Mrs. Zipoti were given plaques. They stood to receive them, and the applause went on and on. Maybe forever, it seemed to Border, but just then Mrs. Zipoti raised her hand and it stopped.

Yes, Mrs. Zipoti.

She nodded approval. The women sat down. Border saw Connie run her hands slowly over the plaque, touching the letters.

More speeches, a few tunes from the school band. Border took off his tie. The sun was high overhead, and he was too warm. Wished he'd worn something else.

"We have a wonderful surprise," he heard the mayor say. "Two of our own have just returned from the Gulf!" A couple of guys in uniform ran up on the stage, each waving a flag. The crowd went wild, worse than before. The high school band played two more pieces, while the soldiers soaked up the applause. Border clapped for a while, then looked at his watch. One more hour at least, then they'd picnic at Connie and Paul's. Man, he was hungry.

The soldiers were given chairs on stage. Another tune from the band. Border tapped on his thighs.

"On to our next order of business," said the mayor, and the program moved along. Border looked around, saw Dana and Jacob. Then he spotted Paul, standing with Connie's son Jeff and Jeff's family, all eyes on the stage.

Presentation of checks. "These will be on display for the next month in the courthouse atrium," said the mayor. There was the old man, waiting his turn. Mrs. McQuillan went forward, handed over her cardboard, shook the mayor's hand.

"Representing the hospital nurses, Crosby Baker."

Right away Border heard grumbling, a low, troubled swell. It caught him by surprise. But why, why be surprised?

Out of the grumbling, clear voices.

"Get the traitor off the stage!"

"Dumbo Gumbo, go back to Canada!"

"Who let him up there? Get him off, get him off!"

"He shouldn't be on the same stage as real soldiers!"

"Shouldn't be on the same planet!"

The grumbling got louder, rolled into a snowball of boos, hisses, and shouts.

The old man stepped forward with his check.

Splat! Someone threw a snow cone. Purple ice hit his shoulder and splashed up on his face. People cheered at that. The mayor froze; time for a leader. What to do?

Border's dad stood smiling while the calls continued. Stood there, taking it. Just taking it. His eyes looked over the crowd; at last he found Border. Bigger smile, eyebrows raised.

Border got the message: Now it's my turn.

The old man took a breath and straightened his shoulders. A clump of grape ice fell out of his hair and slid down his face. People laughed — now he was a traitor *and* a fool. He wiped his face, wiped his shirt, wiped his hands.

A single clear voice: "It's coward's blood on his shirt!"

Border pushed forward. Good to be big; people got out of the way.

Straight to the stage. "What's this?" said the mayor.

"Excuse me, sir," said Border. "Hey, Dad," he called and took off his suit coat, unbuttoned his shirt, handed them both to his father. "Here, take mine."

Standing bare-chested, he heard the first whistle, then there were more. Catcalls, yoo-hooing. Finally, his name: "Yeah, Border!" He looked at the crowd. Did he dare?

Yes.

Border lifted his arms and flexed.

Almost a riot. Cheers and applause exploded into a roar. Border grinned, looked around.

Hey, miracles happen: Mrs. Zipoti and Connie — struck dumb.

The noise continued until the shirts were exchanged and rebuttoned. Border leaned and whispered to his father. "They love us, Dad."

The old man shook his head and smiled. "They love you."

Family Picture —

Party at Connie and Paul's. Border's the last one there. It was hard leaving the courthouse because so many people wanted to talk, shake his hand, slap his back. Ha, ha, kid, you shut up those bums. Then he had to go home to change. Jeans and a T-shirt. It's a holiday, after all.

In the kitchen, the phone machine blinks, a message from Mom. He'll call back later, share the story. Okay, so you no longer love him, he'll tell her, but the way he just took it — you would have been proud.

Across the street, the yard is crowded. Music playing, people dancing. Border's stomach growls. Where's the food?

He sees Paul and Dana putting platters on a table. She turns, gives an order to Jacob, who's right there. Liz leads her sisters through the crowd and deposits them with her parents before walking away. Mrs. McQuillan hugs one of the girls. Border sees his father standing against a tree, talking to Connie's kid, who has his arms around his wife. The old man slips a hand into Maggie's.

The music gets louder. Border grins. Connie's favorite tape, her traveling songs. Everyone laughs, the mob in the yard shifts, and for a moment he sees Connie and Mrs. Zipoti dancing. Arms raised, hips rocking, while Aretha sings on.

"There you are," Dana says. "You took so long. Everyone's here. We were going to take a family picture, but the coals were ready and we couldn't wait. Oh, Jacob, we need the cooler!" She rushes off, Jacob follows.

Family picture? And who's in it? Border frowns. He's never agreed with his mother and her friends, who preach that a family is born any time people live together. Leave one, start another. Too easy, Mom.

All these friends, though. It's something.

There's a crash and all eyes turn to the house. An embarrassed face grimaces behind the door's glass.

"Open it first!" someone shouts.

"Just like my dog," someone else says.

Border laughs in agreement. Just like old Pooch. Catches his breath. Yeah, that's it. That's what it is. Everyone here — okay, they aren't his family. Take any picture you want, but don't call it a family picture. Still, it's something. Something like Pooch must have felt, what went through her mind, her little dog brain, when she heard everyone come home at the end of a day. Charge the door, welcome them back. *Woof woof, woof woof, ah-rooo.*

That's it. Thanks, Pooch.

Woof woof, woof woof, my people.

MARSHA QUALEY is the author of four young-adult novels, including *Come in from the Cold, Everybody's Daughter,* and *Revolutions of the Heart.* She lives in northern Minnesota with her husband, four children, three cats, and a dog.

Thought-Provoking Novels
from Today's Headlines

HOMETOWN
by Marsha Qualey   72921-0/$3.99 US/$4.99 Can

Border Baker isn't happy about moving to his father's rural
Minnesota hometown, where they haven't forgotten that
Border's father fled to Canada rather than serve in Vietnam.
Now, as a new generation is bound for the Persian Gulf, the
town wonders about the son of a draft dodger.

NOTHING BUT THE TRUTH
by Avi   71907-X/$4.50 US /$5.99 Can

Philip was just humming along with *The Star Spangled
Banner*, played each day in his homeroom. How could this
minor incident turn into a major national scandal?

TWELVE DAYS IN AUGUST
by Liza Ketchum Murrow   72353-0/$3.99 US/$4.99 Can

Sixteen-year-old Todd is instantly attracted to Rita Beckman,
newly arrived in Todd's town from Los Angeles. But when
Todd's soccer teammate Randy starts spreading the rumor that
Rita's twin brother Alex is gay, Todd isn't sure he has the
courage to stick up for Alex.

THE HATE CRIME
by Phyllis Karas   78214-6/$3.99 US/$4.99 Can

Zack's dad is the district attorney, so Zack hears about all
kinds of terrible crimes. The latest case is about graffiti defac-
ing the local temple. But it's only when Zack tries to get to the
bottom of this senseless act that he fully understands the terror
these vicious scrawls evoke.